Sherlock Holmes:
In Search of the Source

Sherlock Holmes:
In Search of the Source

Jeff Falkingham

To order additional copies of this book, contact:
Xlibris Corporation
1-888-795-4274
www.Xlibris.com
Orders@Xlibris.com
54778

CONTENTS

IN MEMORY OF

Jacob Vradenberg Brower
Jan. 21, 1844-June 1, 1905
Archaeologist, Historian

Jane Grey Swisshelm
Dec. 6, 1815-July 22, 1884
Journalist, Crusader

ON THE COVER: Firefighters and gawkers look on as a steam-powered pump on a horse-drawn wagon sprays water onto the burned-out Schutte Building at the southwest corner of East Seventh Street and Jackson in lowertown St. Paul, Minnesota, on the morning of December 19, 1896. Original photo by John H. Dickey, digitally enhanced by Randy Meyers. Photos on this page and the cover used with permission of the Minnesota Historical Society.

LowerTown

St. Paul, Minnesota ~ 1896

NOTE: MAP NOT DRAWN TO SCALE. DISTANCES TO LEFT & RIGHT ARE GREATER THAN THEY APPEAR.

BOARDMAN HOTEL = E	IMPROVEMENT ARCH = Q	POLICE HQ = G
FOLEY'S BILLIARDS = H	MAGEE'S SALOON = O	RYAN HOTEL = N
GRAND OLD INN = A	METRO OPERA HOUSE = M	SCHUTTE BLDG. = P
GROCH'S CAFÉ = F	NEWSPAPER ROW = L	SEVEN CORNERS = C
HAMM'S BREWERY = S	NINA CLIFFORD'S = D	STATE CAPITOL = J
HILL MANSION = B	NORTH STAR BREWERY = R	WHITE HOUSE = K

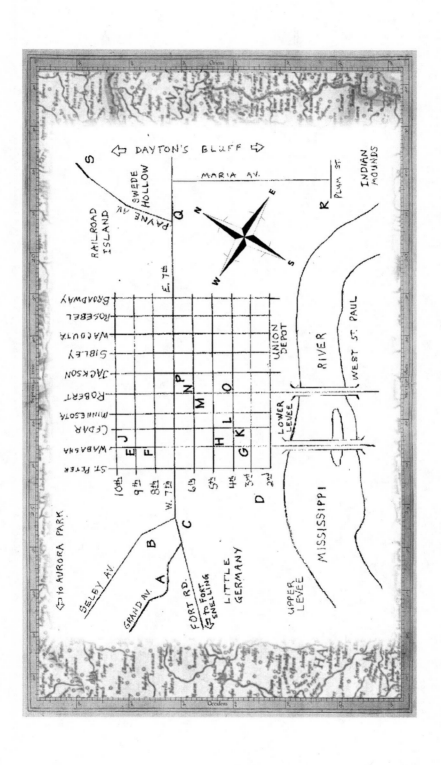

CHAPTER 1

RUDE AWAKENING

It felt like I'd barely fallen asleep, when I was shaken from my slumber.

"Peter, wake up," the voice said. In less than a moment, I realized the speaker was Holmes.

"Wake up, Peter," he repeated. "The desk clerk was just here with a message."

"Again?" I said groggily. "What is it now?"

"It's from the Superintendent," Holmes explained. "After the fire, they found a body in his storeroom—a dead body. He wants to see us right away."

"What time is it?" I asked, as I struggled to my feet.

"Just after seven."

No wonder I was groggy. I'd gotten to bed less than two hours earlier. I hadn't bothered to get undressed, which made it easy to get ready now. Within minutes, we had raced down to Seven Corners, hopped on a streetcar, and reached the Schutte Building. Nels Sandberg, the night watchman, was there to greet us.

"The Superintendent will be tied up with the press for a few more minutes," Sandberg said. "He asked me to take you down to the basement right away."

He led us to a back stairwell and pointed us down a long hallway. Near the end of the hall, we found a young foot patrolman. The nametag on his dark blue uniform said O'Harra.

"Yup, I'm the one who found the body," he said proudly, in response to our question. "Being the new guy on the squad, little Daniel O'Harra was sent to search the basement. Nothing to find down here but sewer rats, they figured. But I fooled them.

I made the biggest find of all: not only the source of the fire, but also a dead body. Imagine my surprise!"

"Any idea on how it came about?" Holmes asked politely.

"Well, I'm just a rookie on this job, but what happened here seems quite clear to me," the young man proposed, puffing up his chest.

"This vagrant," he said, with a jerk of his thumb, "broke in the door here, as you can plainly see. He rifled the drawers and cupboards, looking for something he could pawn for booze money. When he didn't find anything, he stopped to light a ciggy, accidentally set fire to the papers he'd scattered, and tried to escape through that overhead window in the corner, by climbing on the chair there.

"With his wooden leg and all, he slipped and fell, hit his head on the window sill, knocked himself out, and died from inhaling the smoke. That's about it, case closed," he said proudly.

"Yes, an open-and-shut case, it certainly would appear," Holmes said, looking over the man's shoulder at the body in the far corner of the room. "I hope your superiors have complimented you on your very thorough deductive technique?"

"Oh, I'm sure they will!" the rookie said. "Truth be told, though, they haven't been here yet. The chief of detectives was on his way out of town for the weekend, but soon as he heard there was a dead body found, he started to hightail it back. He'll be here within the hour, they tell me. In the meantime, I'm not to let anybody touch a thing."

"Oh, I would never presume to touch anything," Holmes said. "I am, in fact, a detective back in my home country of England, and I don't believe I've ever run across a foot patrolman as intuitive as yourself. Are you sure I can't just take a quick look around the premises? Perhaps a bit of your American ingenuity and superior skills will rub off on me."

Patrolman O'Harra, though obviously flattered, wasn't buying it. "I'm sorry, sir. The only person I'm allowed to let examine this room, and that would be for insurance purposes only, is the tenant himself."

"That would be me," said the Superintendent, who had come up behind us. "This gentleman is my trusted associate. If I remain here, in your presence, would it be permissible for him to take inventory of the room on my behalf?"

The young patrolman now found himself outnumbered, by a pair of very smooth talkers, and eventually relented. "OK, one of you can go in, to take a careful look around," he said. "The other two need to stay out here with me. We don't want the chief of detectives to think I let a herd of buffaloes run around in there."

Holmes eased through the doorway, and began to move very slowly around the perimeter of the room. His hands were folded behind his back, making it obvious he intended to disturb nothing in sight. Though at times his body was totally still, his eyes were constantly moving, up and down, left and right, taking measure of every square inch. When he finally reached the corpse, he looked back at me, made a tiny nod toward the patrolman, and I got the hint. I elbowed the Superintendent, who picked up on it immediately. Together, we did our best to distract the young policeman, while Holmes did what he could to examine the dead body.

Before we knew it, we heard Holmes coughing. He was standing just a few feet from us. "I'm sorry," he said, between coughs. "I seem to be momentarily overcome by the smoke. Peter, do you think you could bring me a small container of water, from that washroom down the hall? I need to quench my thirst."

I wasn't sure what he was up to, but I did as he asked. I found the janitor's coffee cup, rinsed it out, and filled it with fresh water. When I handed it to Holmes, he put the tin cup to his lips, promptly coughed again, and spilled the water on the floor.

"I'm so sorry," he said again, still coughing. "I'll clean it up." He quickly pulled a large handkerchief from his pocket, spread it out flat on the floor, and patted it down, before carefully folding it once and tucking it inside his coat.

"OK, that's it, you'll all have to leave now, before you make a bigger mess of things," Patrolman O'Harra said.

Holmes, having gotten nearly everything he wanted, nodded in compliance. Before we left, he had one final question for the young rookie.

"Have you identified the victim yet?"

"No, sir, he didn't have a thing on him. For now, he'll go into the book as a John Doe."

"When you get around to trying to find out who he was," Holmes offered, "start with small print shops in the area. His misshapen hand suggests a long career as a type compositor."

With that, we left the befuddled young man behind and headed toward the stairs, the elevator shaft being roped off, yet another victim of the fire. When we got outside, I had a question for Holmes: "Is it him?"

"Is what whom?" Holmes responded.

"The dead man with a wooden leg," I said excitedly. "Is it Jonathan Small, from the Agra treasure, in Sign of the Four?"

"Of course not," Holmes replied. "Small escaped from prison, and died on a boat to Brazil. Besides, Small lost his right leg, above the knee. This unfortunate soul is missing his left leg, below the knee. A careful reader, and writer, would have noted the difference."

"Well, sure, I noticed," I said. "I just thought Mr. Watson could have gotten it mixed up in his story."

"He has a keener eye than that," Holmes admonished me.

"It's not his eyes I'm worried about, it's his memory," I said. "He can't even remember if he himself was shot in the shoulder or the leg."

Holmes eyed me for a moment, then said quietly, "Watson has registered some criticism of your writing, as well."

"You let him read it, too?" I asked. "What did he say? I'd really like to know."

"Another time, perhaps," Holmes said, shaking his head. "Right now, I have to figure out who murdered the poor man we just saw."

"Did you say murder?" asked the Superintendent, who had caught up with us once again. "What makes you say that?"

"There are too many holes in Patrolman O'Harra's theory," said Holmes. "The victim was indeed a vagrant, but that's where the story falls apart. With only one good leg, he couldn't possibly have broken in the door. He came in through the window, most likely looking for a place to get warm. The man's body was facing the back of the chair, not the window. That means he was probably using the chair as cover, not as a ladder. There is no blood on the window sill, and its smooth surface doesn't match the pattern of the wound on his forehead. There are freshly broken bones in the left wrist and two fingers of the right hand, indicating he was trying to defend himself from a blow—a very severe blow, judging from the fracture in his skull. His teeth and gums show he was a chewer, not a smoker, of tobacco. And the fire was set on purpose, as evidenced by two things: All of the papers were piled in the center of the room, not scattered about. And there was the faint smell of kerosene in the air, yet all of the lamps in the building are electric."

"Good Lord," said the Superintendent, shaking his head at Holmes' acumen. "What does it all mean?"

"It means," Holmes summarized, "that someone else broke into the storeroom, killed the man who was already there with a vicious blow to the head, ransacked the room to make it look like a burglary, and set the place afire, using liquid fuel from a container he then took from the room with him—along with the murder weapon."

"Anything else?" I asked, my brain already drowning in puzzlement.

"Only that our killer is over six feet tall, above average in weight, and left-handed," Holmes replied. "It will be a few hours before I can tell you where he works. After that, he should be in custody by the end of the day."

Amazingly, Holmes was right on every count but one: the timeline. It took five days to find and apprehend the killer. Before I tell you that story, I'd like to take you back a day and a half, to the evening of December 17, 1896.

CHAPTER 2

A REUNION

"Here, boy," the voice said, as I felt a coin pressed into my palm. "Now, if you would be so kind . . ."

I looked down at the grubby old ha'penny in my hand, then up into the grayest eyes I'd ever seen. We both burst into laughter, appreciating this brief reenactment of our initial meeting.

"It's great to see you again, sir," I said, shaking his hand vigorously.

"You, too, Petey—or don't they call you Petey anymore?" he asked.

"Ma and Pa still do, but most folks call me Peter now," I replied. I was twenty-two years old, after all; twenty-two and a half, actually.

"Then I shall call you Peter, too. And you may call me Holmes," he offered. That will take some getting used to, I thought to myself.

Once again, Sherlock Holmes had snuck up behind me at a train station. Ten years earlier, it had been on a nearly deserted wooden walkway outside a makeshift depot in the tiny border town of Browns Valley, Minnesota. This time, it was on a busy concrete platform at Union Depot in the state's booming capital city of St. Paul.

"Where are we off to?" he asked, as we picked up his bags.

"The Ryan Hotel," I answered. "I know you enjoy the hustle and bustle of big city life, so I've booked you a room smack dab in the center of it all. It's only a few blocks away. Why don't we throw your bags on their carriage, and walk? It's such a nice evening."

It's true. Though Christmas was barely a week away, temperatures on this very pleasant Thursday had hovered in the 30s most of the day. Not for long, though. Today's newspaper

16

warned of a cold spell that could plunge us into sub-zero temps by the weekend.

"Have you eaten?" I asked, as we checked his bags with the Ryan's amiable porter.

"Not since Chicago," he said.

"Good. I know a place along the way: Magee's, near Fourth and Robert. They run a soup and sandwich special on weekday evenings. And it's only two blocks from your hotel."

As we stepped out onto Third Street, I thought of how a trip to the train station had always filled up my senses. I loved the sight of the huge locomotives, their big wheels glistening from constant contact with the rails. I thrilled at the sound of their whistles, the hiss of their steam, the conductor's "All aboard!" I even liked the smell of the wood they burned as fuel.

That was in Browns Valley, in the 1880s. Here in St. Paul, in 1896, one thing had changed. The pleasant smell of charred wood had been replaced by the pungent odor of burning coal. That, and the aroma of hundreds of disembarking passengers who'd been crammed together on the train, wearing the same clothes for days and not bathing for a week. Not to mention the stench of dung and urine left on the street by the line of horses waiting for their carriages to fill up.

But a few brisk blocks in the evening air would cleanse my senses, and bring back my appetite, I was sure!

"So, how are things in Browns Valley?" he asked.

"Great!" I replied. "You won't believe how much it's grown since the Indian lands across the border opened up to white settlement a few years back. There must be seven hundred people living there now, with half as many more coming and going through town every day."

"Really," he said, as if not very impressed.

"Oh, yeah," I said, trying to sound more enthusiastic. "Everything they had one or two of when you were there, they have three or four of now. Banks, saloons, hardware stores, dry goods stores, blacksmiths, lumber yards, harness shops, half a dozen land offices. They even have an opera house—and a roller skating rink, too!"

"You don't say!" he said, mocking my enthusiasm. "And your folks, how are they?"

"They're fine. Pa moved his barbershop back into the old courthouse, beneath our home. And he took on a partner again. Actually, he's taken on a series of them. He no sooner gets them trained in, he says, than they go out on their own. But he doesn't mind. Most of them try to get a customer in and out as fast as they can, while Pa, you know, he likes to make a social event out of it."

"Yes, I remember," Holmes acknowledged with a grin. "And your mother, how is she?"

"Oh, she's doing great, now that she's finally gotten used to missing me," I laughed. "Several years back, she started doing volunteer work at the school, helping them set up a library in a basement corner of the Literary Hall. Over the years, it developed into a full-time job, with the school paying half her wages and the town paying the other half. I think she's happier now than she's ever been—especially with the wedding coming up."

"Ah, yes, the wedding," Holmes said. "You'll have to tell me all about it over dinner. When do I get to meet the blushing bride?"

"Tomorrow night," I answered. "Her ladies' singing group will be part of the Schubert Club program at the Metropolitan Opera House, half a block from your hotel. We'll have dinner with her afterward, and she can tell you all about the wedding herself, if you don't mind."

"Perfect," he said. "And when do we get to meet this famous future father-in-law of yours?"

I had wondered when that was coming. Just as I'd wondered whether Holmes had actually come back to Minnesota for the sole purpose of attending my wedding, or more for the opportunity it afforded him to meet the famous Jacob V. Brower.

"He's not really her father," I explained. "She calls him that, and he's always treated her like his own daughter. But he's her uncle, and her guardian. Her own parents are dead."

"I'm sorry," Holmes said. "How did they die?"

"In a train wreck, near Willmar, around 1880," I explained. "Becky was only five years old. She was staying with her aunt and uncle at the time, and they just kept her. They already had two kids of their own, so she fit right in. Anyhow, we'll be having lunch with him tomorrow, in his office, which is also right around the corner from your hotel."

"It seems you've thought of everything, then," Holmes said, at last sounding at least a bit impressed. "Now, Peter, tell me what you've been up to these past ten years, and how you ended up where you are today."

I told him how, after finishing school in Browns Valley, I'd gone on to the Normal College in St. Cloud, with the intention of becoming a teacher. I soon learned that I didn't have the patience to work with young kids. But I did have a talent, and a passion, for writing. So after two years in St. Cloud, I went on to journalism school at the University of Minnesota, in hopes of becoming a writer. After two more years of training there, I returned to St. Cloud to serve a six-month apprenticeship with the St. Cloud Times. I had just completed that, and in two weeks, I was about to start my career as a cub reporter with the St. Paul Dispatch.

"I'll be doing O's and B's at first," I said. "That's obituaries and birth announcements, along with weddings, engagements, anniversaries, that sort of thing. Yeah, it's boring, I know! As soon as I get my feet wet, I hope to move on to the crime beat. My teachers at the university tell me that, once I make a name for myself in the newspaper business, it will be easier to get my book published."

"Your book?" he asked.

"Yeah, the one I wrote for my final project in college. The story of our adventure together, the first time you were here."

"Ah, the manuscript you sent me," he mused.

"Oh, you got it then? You never replied."

"I wasn't aware it required a response," he said.

"Did you read it?" I asked.

"Of course," he nodded.

"What did you think of it?"

Holmes paused for a minute. Then he spoke carefully. "The account was accurate enough, I suppose. As for your own role in the story, it was interesting to be able to perceive things from your point of view. As for my role, there were many things going on of which you were not aware."

"Like what?" I asked.

Holmes shook his head. "It matters little. By now, I'm used to having others put their twist on a tale. By the time Scotland Yard tells their side of a story to the press, and they in turn relay it to the public, I can barely recognize the case as something I might have worked on. Even Watson is occasionally guilty of putting his own slant on things. But here we are at Magee's, I believe!"

And that was the end of that discussion (at least for now).

CHAPTER 3

THE SHADOW

A mong food and liquor aficionados in lowertown St. Paul, Magee's had a reputation for providing "all things good for all good men (and women)." In his nearly twenty-five years in the saloon business, Mr. Magee had built up a loyal following. On weekends, his restaurant was the type of place where you could take your wife, or fiancée, for an elegant dining experience on a special occasion. During the week, he catered to the working crowd, with good food and man-sized drinks, at prices that wouldn't break your budget, whether you were a working stiff on a night out with your pals, or a salesman plying a prospective client. Catered is the operative word there, as he specialized in delivering noontime box lunches to dozens of busy workers in the many office buildings nearby.

On weekends, Magee's tables were covered with white linen, and lit with fancy candles. On weeknights, though, the dark walnut tables were bare, ready for a slightly rougher crowd. A recent expansion to the kitchen, to keep up with the catering business, had reduced the size of the barroom. But the addition of mirrors on all the walls made the room seem bigger than it actually was.

We found a corner table away from the bar, ordered a couple of beers, and perused the menu.

"So tell me more about the inhabitants of your hometown," Holmes said, after we ordered our sandwiches. "How are the Browns? Are they all doing well?"

"Big Guy Sam is busier than ever," I said. "He's involved in land sales with his little brother, Joe Junior, and Mr. Renville. The latter two spend most of their time in the field, checking on land, and meeting with customers. Sam stays behind and handles most of the paper work. Little Guy Sam does the leg work for him, running to the bank, post office, attorneys, register of deeds, whatever. They're probably the biggest real estate dealer in town right now."

"The Widow Brown, is she still alive?" Holmes asked.

"Oh, yeah, I sometimes hear her plunking away at the piano when I go by."

"And Pheebs?"

"She got engaged recently, too, to a fellow by the name of Eddington. I don't know much about him, but she seems real happy," I told him.

"Good for her! And the others? Muley, Iron Will, Mr. Milles?"

I took a moment to gather my thoughts as the waitress delivered our food. Then I answered his questions, to the best of my recollection. I really didn't get back to Browns Valley as often as I should.

"Henry Milles is still alive, and still telling tales," I said. "Though he sometimes forgets where he's at in the story, and has to start over. He's in his nineties now, I'm sure. Muley married a gal from the reservation. He has his own blacksmith shop now, in the new town of Sisseton, near the foot of the coteau in South Dakota. William Patterson, I'm afraid, is dead. Old Iron Will stepped into the middle of a dispute over a land claim, and one of the parties whipped out a pistol and shot him, right through the temple, some five years ago now."

"I'm very sorry to hear that," he said. He paused for a moment, then said quietly, "Peter, look over my left shoulder, at the mirror behind me, and tell me if you recognize that man at the far end of the bar, the one in the dark green stocking cap."

"The one filling his pipe just now?" I asked.

"Yes, that's the one. Do you know him?"

"No, I don't think so. Why?"

"He looks vaguely familiar to me," Holmes said. "As I have few acquaintances here, I was thinking he might be someone from your past."

I studied the man's reflection for another minute before I replied. "Nope, I've never seen him before in my life."

"Well, I have," Holmes said decidedly.

"Where, do you recall?"

"Not right now—but I will," he said. "At the moment, my mind is filled with memories of our old friends in Browns Valley. Once I set those images aside, others will emerge from the nooks and crannies. Your mind can only process so much data at once, you know."

"Well, if you really want to know who he is, you could always ask him," I suggested.

"Oh, I will, without a doubt," Holmes replied. "But not until I know more about him. Like a good barrister, a competent detective rarely asks a question for which he does not already know the answer."

While I pondered that for a moment, Holmes changed the subject. "So tell me, Peter, how did you and your fiancée meet?"

"We met at Itasca State Park, three summers ago, after my first year at Normal. Mr. Brower was park superintendent at the time. Becky was working in the lodge. I was playing in the band, and she caught my eye."

"You play in a band?" Holmes interrupted.

"Sure, the Browns Valley Brass Band."

"When did that start?" Holmes asked.

"Oh, quite a few years ago now," I explained. "When Pa joined the band, Mr. Barrett gave him an old cornet from his store as a gift. It was always lying around the house, so one day I picked it up, and found out I was pretty good at it. After a few years, they asked me to sit in with the band."

"And your father, does he still play?"

"Yeah, we play together. It's been fun," I said. "Of course, since I started college, I can only play with them during the summer, and on holidays. But once a year they take a big road trip, and that year we played at Itasca."

"Where, as you say, this young lady caught your eye. And you approached her?"

"I didn't have the nerve," I admitted sheepishly. "She came up to me, while the band was taking a break."

"And she broke the ice by complimenting you on your chops, I presume?"

"No," I said, laughing at his use of the lingo. "She said, 'You're the writer, aren't you?' As I said, it was after my first year in St.

23

Cloud. I'd just had one of my short stories published in the school literary quarterly. It was about you and me, and our first test run on the ice sled. So, I guess you could say that you brought us together."

"You're welcome," Holmes said. "Now, I must ask you to do something for me."

"What's that?" I asked.

"I recall now where I've seen our new friend before," he answered. "He was waiting at the depot when I got off the train. And he was lurking nearby as we dealt with the carriage driver from the hotel. Once we've finished eating, I'm going to lay some money on the table to pay the bill, then shake your hand and go out the front door. You sit here as if you're waiting for change, and see if he follows me. Be discreet, use the mirrors."

"You got it," I said. Amid more small talk, we finished our meal. Then, as planned, we paid the bill, shook hands, and Holmes headed for the front door. Sure enough, the man at the end of the bar got up and followed him out. I hadn't spent more than a minute or two pondering my next move, before Holmes came up behind me.

"Did he take the bait?" Holmes asked.

"Like a fish," I replied, "hook, line and sinker."

Holmes immediately rushed to the bar, grabbed the man's beer glass, held it up to the light, then passed it under his nostrils, before handing it back to the startled bartender. My friend then wetted the tip of his finger, touched it first to the bar, then to his nose, and finally to his tongue. When he nodded toward the front door, I scurried to meet him. Just as we reached the entrance, the man in the dark green tuque opened the door from the other side.

"Danke," said Holmes, bowing ever so slightly. Then, "Guten Abend!"

As the two of us headed up Robert Street toward the Ryan Hotel, the startled stranger still stood in front of Magee's, the door, and his jaws, both held wide open.

"What was that all about?" I asked, as we crossed Fifth Street.

"From his choice of ale, and the speck of tobacco he spilled on the bar while filling his pipe, the man is clearly German,"

Holmes explained, "so I spoke to him in his native language. That ought to give him something to wonder about."

"I still think you should confront him," I said.

"Oh, I shall, you can be certain of that," Holmes replied, "but all in due time, my friend, all in due time. There will be plenty of other opportunities, of that I have no doubt."

As usual, Sherlock Holmes had hit the nail right on the head.

CHAPTER 4

PIG'S EYE

If you discount the fur trappers and buyers who moved about the territory, the first real settlers in Minnesota were the traders who supplied whiskey to the soldiers at Fort Snelling (and occasionally, illegally, to the Indians nearby) in the early 1820s. When these squatters were kicked off the military reservation, they moved a couple of miles down the Mississippi River, to a landing already occupied by another of their kind, one Pierre Parrant, also known as Pig's Eye. Were it not for a Catholic priest named Father Galtier, who in 1841 built on this levee a small log chapel he christened The Basilica of Saint Paul, the settlement that came to be known as Saint Paul Landing (and, eventually, as the city of St. Paul) might still be called Pig's Eye. Wouldn't that be a hoot?

Anyhow, it was the lowertown district of the city of St. Paul, not Pig's Eye, to which I treated Sherlock Holmes to a guided walking tour on the morning of Friday, December 18, 1896—a date we will always remember, for reasons you will soon see.

When we arrived at the Ryan Hotel after our late supper at Magee's on Thursday night, my friend's bags were already in his room. He was surprised, and somewhat disappointed, I think, to learn that I would not be staying at the Ryan. Instead, I had a room at the Grand Old Inn, near Seven Corners, a short streetcar ride to the west.

The Ryan, I told him, like the St. Paul Hotel on Fifth Street and St. Peter, was reserved for royalty, visiting dignitaries, and first-time guests in our city. Regulars like myself, along with traveling salesmen and people with families, stayed at the Merchants Hotel or at the Grand (though the Old part of the name was much more accurate). In reality, it was a matter of cost. Mr. Brower was picking up the tab for Holmes, in return for the honor of meeting the famous detective and having him as a guest at his daughter's wedding. My room at the Grand was a wedding gift from long-time family friend Fred Dittes, who regularly kept a room there because, for many years, his grain elevator in Travare supplied all the wheat for the hotel's bakery, home of the famous Grand Old Inn Cracked-Wheat Bread.

Anyhow, I met Holmes early that morning, and told him of my strategy for our tour.

"When we left the Union Depot concourse last night, we first walked west on Third Street," I explained. "Because it's barely a hundred yards from the water, and runs parallel to the river for several blocks, Third Street used to be the heart of the city, when steamboats served the levee. Once the railroads took over, people wanted to get away from the noise and the soot, and the center of commerce moved all the way up to Seventh Street.

"You probably noticed last night, about all that remains on Third Street now, besides the depot, are freight offices and train sheds, a couple of horse stables, several warehouses, the St. Paul volunteer fire department, and one or two cheap hotels, for transients who can't afford to go anywhere else."

"It did seem pretty dismal," Holmes agreed.

"Once we turned north on Robert Street," I pointed out, "you started to see some of the more established businesses: banks, restaurants and so on. Robert was the second street to get a bridge across the river. The first was Wabasha Street, which we'll see later this morning. Both bridges take you to the textile and garment manufacturers in what's known as West St. Paul, though it's actually due south of here."

"For a small-town boy, you sure know a lot about the big city," Holmes said.

"Well, once I decided I wanted to be a journalist, St. Paul became the pinnacle for me," I told him. "Minneapolis might be the flour milling capital of the world, but St. Paul is the home of the state government, where all the important decisions are made, and it's the financial and commercial center of the entire region. While I was at the university, I spent a lot of free time exploring this city, learning what makes it tick, so I could someday get a job here. And, what do you know, it worked!"

"So, what's the plan?" he asked, as we walked out of the Ryan and onto Sixth Street.

"I think we'll continue up Robert to Seventh Street, walk east to Rosebel, south to Fourth, west to Wabasha or St. Peter, north to Seventh, and back here to the Schutte Building, to meet Superintendent Brower. In all, it's about a two-mile walk. At a leisurely pace, that should get us back here just in time for lunch."

"Sounds great," said Holmes, and we were off.

"As I mentioned, you're right in the heart of the retail district," I said, as we turned up Robert Street. "On your left is Mannheimer Brothers, famous for its silks and men's furnishings. On your right, just past the Ryan Hotel's pharmacy, is L. G. Hoffman's, specializing in men's hats and furs." They had a sign in the window advertising men's suits for $10 to $15.

As we reached Seventh Street, I motioned kitty-corner. "There's the Golden Rule, the most popular department store in St. Paul, rivaled only by Donaldson's in Minneapolis. As you can see from their signs, Santa Claus will be there every night next week." Across from the Golden Rule, the Emporium was also advertising holiday specials.

Heading east on Seventh Street, I pointed out the Cardozo Furniture Store, between Robert and Jackson. "The furniture store occupies the first two floors of the Schutte Office Building, also known as the Ryan Annex," I explained. "Superintendent Brower's office is on the third floor, with a bunch of dentists—don't ask me how he got mixed up with them!"

As we continued east on Seventh, we passed a number of home furnishing stores, druggists, jewelers, news stands, cigar shops and saloons. With Christmas just a week away, every one of the merchants seemed to be doing a booming business, even early on a Friday morning.

Turning south onto Rosebel, I explained to Holmes that the wags had taken to calling it Wall Street, probably because James J. Hill and all the other railroad barons had their offices at the south end, between Rosebel and Broadway, one block to the east. At the north end, though, we were in the jobbing district, with its boot and shoe manufacturers, saddle and harness shops, dry goods, flour, grain and liquor wholesalers, and so on.

At this point, I made an observation. "I see our tail is still with us," I said.

"Don't worry about him," Holmes replied, "he's harmless."

"How do you know?"

"I checked him out last night. From the window in my room, I noticed a courtyard behind the hotel. After you left and I'd gotten settled in, I took an empty wine bottle I found in the hall, went down to the courtyard, and staggered around in the dark, as if I'd had a few too many. He followed me, of course, but kept his distance. If he'd meant to harm me, he had plenty of opportunity last night. Obviously, he's just keeping an eye on me."

"Why?" I asked.

"That's exactly what I intend to find out," Holmes answered. "Why, and for whom?"

By now we were heading west on Fourth Street. Here, two blocks from the river, the businesses were more industrial in nature: gas and electric companies, coal and rubber suppliers, a boarding house or two, and, of course, the obligatory saloon in the middle of every block. As we passed a couple of lending houses, I realized we were heading back into the financial district. Straight ahead was Newspaper Row.

"See that tall building just ahead, on the right?" I asked him. "That's the Pioneer Press Building. It's thirteen stories high, the tallest building this side of Chicago. It has all the modern conveniences, including four passenger elevators, and one just for freight. They say there are nearly two hundred offices in that building alone."

"Whatever for?" Holmes wanted to know, as we got closer.

"Real estate, land offices, life insurance, fire insurance, investment companies, that sort of thing," I explained. "I told you, St. Paul is the financial and commercial heart of the whole region. Hundreds of deals take place here every day, with thousands and thousands of dollars changing hands, maybe millions."

"That must keep the lawyers busy," Holmes suggested.

"Yes, and a lot of them work out of the Globe Building," I said, pointing to the ten-story building coming up on the left, at Fourth and Cedar. "They're right across the street from the Ramsey County Courthouse and St. Paul's City Hall, which makes it convenient not only for the attorneys, but also for the Globe's reporters."

"And where is your newspaper's office, Peter?"

"We just passed it, back at Fourth and Minnesota," I said. "We'll probably go there tomorrow morning, if you'd like."

By now we'd passed Wabasha and reached St. Peter. Here, we were in the millinery district, home to ladies' tailors, dress- and hat-makers, and fashions. At St. Peter and Fifth, in the Merrill Building, was St. Paul Book and Stationery, across from the afore-mentioned St. Paul Hotel. Just up the street was Litt's Grand Opera House, home of the Twin City Mandolin Orchestra. Beyond that was the arts district, where teachers of music, dance, piano and voice plied their trade—and where Becky hoped to get a job some day.

Doubling back to Wabasha, we passed the Market Place, with their sign boasting of "good warm food, and the city's largest glass of beer." In a city with half a dozen saloons for every four-way intersection, that's quite a boast! Other points of interest included Foley's Billiards Parlor at 450 Wabasha, and, a block up the street, the Eisenmenger Meat Company, which supplied all the meat for Fort Snelling, as well as the dining cars of the Great Northern and Northern Pacific Railroads.

As we reached Schuneman & Evans, another men's furnishings store at Wabasha and Sixth, we found ourselves back in the heart of the retail district. At Seventh Street, I pointed out the state capitol, three blocks north on Wabasha, before we headed east again. After checking out the holiday sale at Yerxa Brothers Candies, we arrived at the Schutte Building. Our tour of Pig's Eye Landing had gotten us right back where we started, just in time for our luncheon appointment with J. V. Brower.

CHAPTER 5

OL'MAN RIVERS

A s I've said in the past, I've never been a big fan of history. I thought I was done with it when I finished school in Browns Valley. Unfortunately, I had to take a couple of history courses in college as well. Seems as if they want you to be "well rounded" (whatever that means) if you're planning to be a journalist.

From what I've learned, Minnesota history can be summed up in two words: rivers, and railroads. Like the Indians, rivers were here long before the white man came to Minnesota. Rivers were home to the beavers that first attracted French and Canadian fur trappers to this land. Rivers provided the trappers and traders with a way to get around, in their canoes and longboats. Rivers helped the early lumberjacks deliver their logs to the saw mill. Rivers served as landmarks, and as borders, in case of disputes. Once the government treaties opened up Indian lands to white settlement, the Mississippi River enabled thousands of immigrants to come to Minnesota by steamboat.

Years later, railroads helped settlers reach the rich farmlands and forests that weren't readily accessible by river. But in the beginning, it was the rivers that were responsible for sustaining life in this land. Minnesota has plenty of them to brag about: not only the Mississippi, but also the Minnesota (formerly the St. Peter), the Rum, the Crow, the St. Croix, the Cannon, and many, many more. And when it comes to rivers, and their importance to this state, there is no greater expert than Jacob Vradenberg Brower.

The Brouer family (as the name was then spelled) came to New Amsterdam from Holland in the 1640s. "They weren't on the Mayflower," J.V. likes to say, "but they were in its wake!" Brower's

31

immediate family came to Minnesota Territory from Michigan in the 1850s, and settled on farmland in the Mississippi River Valley, north of St. Cloud. When the Dakota Conflict broke out, young Jacob, then 19 years old, enlisted in the First Regiment of Mounted Rangers, and rode the entire length of the Minnesota River Valley with General Sibley. It was then and there that he first became interested in Indian burial rites.

Mustered out of the army in November of 1863, Brower worked briefly in Kansas, where he learned about Coronado's 1541 expedition up the Mississippi River, in search of the ancient civilization of Quivira. Before the end of the Civil War, Brower joined the navy and served aboard Union gunboats on the lower Mississippi, under Admiral Farragut.

Returning to Minnesota after the War Between the States, J. V. married Armina Shava in 1867, and became involved in a number of civic activities. He passed the bar, served briefly in the state legislature, worked as register for the U. S. Land Office in St. Cloud, founded the town of Browerville, ran a couple of small-town newspapers, and got heavily involved with the Minnesota Historical Society.

His efforts to settle a nearly century-old dispute over the source of the Mississippi River led to the establishment of Itasca State Park, resulting in the natural preservation of thousands of acres of virgin forest and pristine waters in northern Minnesota. He also went up the Missouri River, tracing it to a source a hundred miles beyond the one "discovered" by Lewis and Clark in 1805.

For each river that he traveled, he recorded the history of the civilization that grew up around it, documenting the location of hundreds of Indian mounds and dozens of villages and forts, and collecting thousands of artifacts and specimens. Through his interest in the relationship between history, geography and civilization, and the many maps and field books he created, he became one of the nation's premier experts in the field of archaeology.

For this, I called him Ol'Man Rivers, after the nickname the veteran steamboaters had for the Mississippi River. Of course, I never called him that to his face, or anywhere he might hear me! With just family around, I might get by with J. V., as most of his peers called him. Whenever there were others about, which was most of the time, I treated him with the respect he deserved, and called him Superintendent, after the post he'd held as founder and first overseer of Itasca State Park.

Anyway, this is the man I took Sherlock Holmes to meet for lunch that Friday afternoon. As I suspected, the two men hit it off immediately.

"Mr. Holmes, I'm delighted to meet you at last, so glad you could come," Brower said with a grin as we entered his office.

"The pleasure is all mine, sir," Holmes replied. "And please accept my congratulations on the upcoming nuptials. Your daughter is getting a fine young man here."

"Thank you, sir, I appreciate that," the Superintendent said. "I knew he was from good stock the moment she told me he was from Browns Valley. You need to have a lot going for you to survive life in that part of the country. I know that from first-hand experience."

"Ah, yes, your journey up the Minnesota with General Sibley," Holmes said. "Is that when you began to develop your abiding interest in rivers?"

"Oh, no, long before that," Brower said with a chuckle. He pointed out that he was born on the banks of the Saline River in southeastern Michigan, raised on a tributary of the Crow Wing River in central Minnesota, and for nearly twenty-five years had lived near the mighty Mississippi in St. Cloud. Even now, his office in St. Paul was only a few blocks from water.

"As a young boy," Brower explained, "I learned that the stream we were living on in Todd County had for decades served as a boundary between the Dakota and the Ojibwe. That was when I first realized that a river was much more than just a source of water."

"Speaking of sources," Holmes asked, "when, and why, did you develop your passion for searching out the sources of rivers?"

Again, Brower chuckled before he answered. "Like you, Mr. Holmes, I am a man of science, a man of reason, a man in search of indisputable factual data. When we say that a river's source lies at an exact point on a map, we should be able to do so with absolute certainty. Alas, this has not always been the case. Too often, politics, economics and personal vanity factored into the equation."

"Fascinating," said Holmes. "Can you give me an example?"

"Oh, my gosh," Brower said, giving it some thought. "I guess it goes all the way back to 1670. That's the year that King Charles II of England granted a charter to the Hudson Bay Company, giving it exclusive trading rights on all rivers and streams flowing into Hudson Bay—which eventually turned out to be nearly half of Canada!

"When Daniel DuLuth traced the Red River of the North all the way down to Lake Traverse, the Hudson Bay Company claimed control of the eastern part of the Dakota Territories, and most of northwestern Minnesota as well. Had he found the link he was searching for between the Red River and Lake Superior, they'd have owned all of northern Minnesota, not only the fur-trapping rights, but also the valuable pine forests, and later the iron mines as well.

"Moving ahead a century or so," Brower said, "when Thomas Jefferson purchased the Louisiana Territories from France in 1803, America didn't want a repeat of the Hudson Bay fiasco. Because the contract said the purchase included all lands between the Mississippi River and the Missouri River Valley, it became important to determine the sources of those two rivers. So, in 1805, Lewis and Clark were dispatched to find the source of the Missouri, and Zebulon Pike was sent to find the source of the Mississippi.

"Unfortunately," Brower continued, "both fell woefully short. Lewis found a spot in the Beaverhead Mountains of Montana, where three small streams joined to form one larger one, and decided that this was the start of the great Missouri River. He named these three creeks the Jefferson, the Madison and the Gallatin, after the President of the United States and the Secretaries of State and the Treasury, and that was the end of that. Lewis and Clark moved on to the second part of their assignment, to try to find a navigable route to the Pacific Ocean.

"Pike, to his credit, claimed one major accomplishment in Minnesota: he bartered with the natives for the piece of land where Fort Snelling now sits. But he, too, fell short of reaching the source of the Mississippi, in part because his keelboat was too large. For the next several decades, explorer after explorer went up the great river, from Joseph Nicollet to Lewis Cass to Henry Schoolcraft, and a dozen others not worth mentioning. Each tried to extend the boundaries of the Louisiana Purchase as far as they could to the north and the west, to cut into the territory of the British and the French.

"For much the same reason," Brower explained, "Stephen Long was sent up the Minnesota River, to Big Stone Lake and beyond, in 1823. He reported that the land was littered with rocks and boulders, and its trees were of the deciduous variety, not the coniferous trees that the lumber industry valued. For this reason, focus from that point on remained on the Upper Mississippi. In fact, the land of the Minnesota River Valley was deemed so worthless, by comparison, that the government was willing to let the Indians keep it in a series of treaties throughout the 1800s.

"Meanwhile, the debate over the source of the Mississippi continued. Finally, in the late 1880s, the Minnesota Historical Society was given authority to examine eighty years' worth of claims, to investigate those of merit, and to determine, once and for always, which was most valid. I am proud and honored to have been part of that process."

"And while you were at it," Holmes chimed in, "you saw what the loggers were doing to the area, and decided that the headwaters and surrounding forests needed to be protected."

"Yes, the establishment of Itasca State Park was another long battle," Brower said, "but well worth it, in the end."

"As for the source of the Missouri," Holmes asked, "I understand you solved that mystery as well, just this past year?"

"Indeed—but that's another story," Brower replied, "a story that will have to wait until another day, as I believe our lunch has finally arrived." Thank God, I thought to myself!

CHAPTER 6

IDLE CHATTER

The food was from Groch's Café, between Eighth and Ninth on Wabasha, near the state capitol.

"We usually get the boxed ploughman's lunch from Magee's," Brower said, "but I understand you two gentlemen ate there last night, so I thought I'd try something different. Besides, Groch is running his holiday special now, a turkey dinner, complete with cranberry sauce, for fifteen cents a plate. How can you beat that?"

"How, indeed?" Holmes replied. "It looks and smells delicious."

"Then let's have at it!" J.V. said. He got no argument from me.

As we ate, the two men continued to chat.

"I'm interested in the portraits on the wall behind your desk," Holmes said to J. V. "In fact, I believe I recognize one or two of the faces. Are they all people with whom you have worked?"

"Many of them are men who have assisted me, in one way or another, on various projects," the Superintendent confirmed, citing a few examples. "Others are people whose work I admire."

"I notice that two of them are women," Holmes said. "May I ask who they are?"

"The one on the left is Harriet Bishop," Brower said. "She came from Vermont as a very young woman to serve as the city of St. Paul's first public school teacher, before Minnesota was even a territory. The one on the right is Jane Grey Swisshelm, from Pennsylvania, via Kentucky. Back east, she was the first female reporter to sit in the press gallery of the United States

Senate, under the tutelage of Horace Greeley. Later, taking Greeley's advice, she moved west and became a very influential newspaper editor in Minnesota. Both women became leaders in fields previously dominated by men. I put their portraits up to inspire my daughters."

"Did it work?" Holmes asked.

"Fortunately," Brower replied, "both Josie and Becky have chosen to follow in Miss Bishop's footsteps, and become teachers."

"That's very admirable," Holmes said. "Forgive me for asking, but I'm curious as to why you say it's fortunate as well?"

"Mrs. Swisshelm led a remarkable life, and fought for many just causes," Brower said, "but she acquired many enemies over the years. My girls don't need that."

"Speaking of your girls," Holmes said, "Peter tells me I'll get to meet one of them tonight. Will you be joining us?"

"Unfortunately, I can not. I have to attend a meeting of the state historical society. We're planning our fiftieth anniversary."

"Already?" Holmes asked, sounding surprised. "I thought Minnesota wasn't admitted to the Union until 1858."

"Yes, that's when we achieved statehood," Brower confirmed. "But the historical society was formed as soon as Minnesota officially became a Territory, in 1849."

"I see," Holmes said. "Still, that puts your anniversary two or three years away."

"I know, but we have a lot to do," Brower explained. "A few of the founding members are still with us, but many have passed away. Other members, like myself, are getting long in the tooth, and won't be around forever. If we want the organization to have a one-hundredth anniversary, we're going to have to bring in a lot of new blood. We plan to use the occasion of our fiftieth anniversary as a rallying call to new recruits—like young Peter here."

"No offense, sir," Holmes said, "but I think you've got your work cut out for you there. Though he seems to know quite a bit about the subject, Peter has told me more than once that he has little interest in history."

"Nonsense," said Brower. "He has a great eye for detail, and a wonderful knack for putting his thoughts into words. The society could use a man like him—especially a young man, with his whole future ahead of him."

I'd been hoping to stay out of this conversation. Now, it appeared, I had no choice but to speak up. "Thank you, sir," I said to J. V. "I'm honored to hear that you feel that way. I'm just not sure this is the right time for me to get involved in something of that nature. I mean, with the wedding coming up, and me starting a new job and all, . . ."

"Perhaps you're right," Brower said, sounding disappointed. "You do have plenty on your plate at the moment." More than you know, I thought to myself; more than you know.

"Speaking of plates," Holmes said, tapping his dinner dish with a fork, "mine is clean. And it was truly a first-class meal. I can't thank you enough."

"It was my pleasure," Brower said. "I'm so glad you could stop by. Now, I'm afraid, it's almost time for me to get back to work. What are you fellows up to the rest of the afternoon?"

"I'm hoping to meet Becky as soon as she gets to town," I said. "If she has any free time before the concert tonight, there are some last-minute wedding plans we need to go over."

"Well, bring her by, if you have time," Brower said. "Otherwise, I might not get a chance to see her until tomorrow. And you, Mr. Holmes, will you be helping with the wedding plans?"

"Oh, I think that's a little outside my area of expertise," he said with a smile. "I do have a small matter to attend to. Which reminds me: do either of you know if there's a boxing gym in town?"

"Not any more," Brower replied. "Archbishop Ireland got the legislature to ban professional prizefighting throughout the state, about four years ago. Why do you ask?"

Holmes then told the Superintendent about the shadow. "Like a backwater tadpole," Holmes explained, "I seem to have grown a tail since I arrived in town. Judging from his cauliflower ears, his broken nose, chipped teeth and swollen knuckles, the man had a long, though not very illustrious, career as a pugilist. Based on my experience, even after they hang up the gloves, that type usually likes to hang around the ring. I thought a visit to a local gym might be the best place to learn more about him."

"Well, the last time they tried to hold a prizefight in St. Paul, in October of last year, it was in the middle of the Mississippi, on a barge, pulled between two steamboats full of fans," Brower said. "The promoters hoped to circumvent the law by holding it on the river, but Governor Clough put a stop to it. Eventually, I heard, the steamers hauled the fans up the St. Croix, where the fights were held on a landing on the Wisconsin side."

"Didn't the Jockey Club used to hold fights in the amphitheater at the fairgrounds?" I asked.

"Ah, Peter, you do know your history after all," Brower said with a grin. "Yes, throughout the 1880s, prizefighting was very popular in Minnesota. Anyplace that had adequate seating, or even just enough open space for fans to stand, was likely to promote a bout. Here in St. Paul, the Music Hall, Market Hall, the Opera House, even the Jackson Street Roller Rink, all had their heydays as boxing venues. Come to think of it, the last legal prizefight in this city, to my knowledge, was probably held at the Olympic Theater, on Seventh and Jackson, right across the street from where we stand at this moment. That might be a good place for you to start your search, Mr. Holmes—either there, or City Hall."

"What would he find at City Hall?" I asked.

"If I remember correctly," Brower replied, "the city police department used to sponsor a local boxing club. I wouldn't be surprised if they still had a boxing ring in their gym—for training purposes only, of course."

"Of course," Holmes replied, with a knowing grin. We shook hands with the Superintendent, thanked him again for lunch, and headed out into the street. There, we were met with a frigid northwest wind.

"Whoa! It feels like that cold front is moving in," I said, "just like the newspapers predicted. We'd better wear an extra layer tonight. It's gonna be a cold one."

With that, we agreed to go our separate ways for the next few hours. I was anxious to meet with Becky, and Holmes, I knew, was itching to find out who'd been following him, and why. We arranged to meet at the Metropolitan Opera House that evening for the Schubert Club program. Neither of us had the slightest inkling of the other events that lie ahead of us that night.

CHAPTER 7

BECKY LOU

As planned, Holmes and I met that evening at the Metropolitan Opera House. It was the night of the Schubert Club's annual college and university scholarship fund-raiser. Each year, just before Christmas, the local club invited several of the area schools to send a chorus or a glee club, and occasionally a brass or woodwind ensemble, to perform holiday music. The University of Minnesota was represented, as well as many of the private schools: Augsburg, Macalaster, Hamline, St. Olaf, St. Thomas and so on. This was the first time the St. Cloud Normal School had been invited to participate, and Becky was nervous about making a good impression.

She needn't have worried. Her group was one of the last to perform in the opening segment of the program. Their first number was warmly received by the audience. The second, in which Becky had a small solo, brought the house to its feet.

"Your fiancée has a lovely voice," Holmes said to me during the intermission. "Have you considered singing together at your wedding?"

"Thanks," I shrugged, "but I can't sing."

"Nonsense," Holmes replied. "Anyone can sing. It's innate."

"You're kidding, right?"

"Not at all," he said. "As Darwin noted, man could carry a tune long before he could carry on a conversation. Of course, some have not yet fully developed the skill, or learned how to utilize it. But all men have it. It's part of Human Nature."

"It's what sets us apart from the animals, then?" I asked.

"Not really. Birds can sing. Wolves howl at the moon. I could give you a dozen other examples, but that's not the point. You can sing. You just have to put your mind to it."

I thought about that for a moment. But I still had my doubts. Besides, the music for our wedding was already set in stone. A few college classmates from Becky's singing group were going to perform a song. Her childhood piano teacher, Sister Armella, was going to play the organ. And, to humor me, a couple of the boys from the Browns Valley Brass Band were going to join her on the processionals as we marched in and out. That was it, far as I knew.

The second half of the Schubert Club program was as enjoyable as the first. It started with a bit of comic relief, as the Elks Club Banjo Band played a few novelty tunes with a holiday theme. Then, each of the groups that had performed earlier came on stage, one right after another, to form a huge mass choir and orchestra that filled the building with beautiful music.

Afterward, Holmes and I retired to the lobby bar to wait for Becky to change out of her costume. As we watched the happy crowd disperse into the street, I caught a glimpse of our new friend, lurking outside the door.

"I see your tail is still with you," I said to Holmes.

"Herr Mueller?" Holmes replied. "Don't worry. As I told you, he's harmless."

"Oh, you know his name now?" I asked in surprise.

"Yes, his name is Klaus Mueller. He was once a fairly well-known prizefighter. You can find his likeness in photos or lithographs on the wall at any number of local establishments—as I did this very afternoon. Apparently, his record was never much to boast about, but he always put up a good fight. I understand he was a real crowd-pleaser, especially among his fellow German immigrants."

"Have you spoken with him?" I asked.

"No," Holmes replied, shaking his head. "As long as he's no trouble, I don't want to blow his cover. It appears he's a bit down on his luck at the moment, and can use the extra money."

"Do you know who he's working for, then?"

"I have a very strong suspicion," Holmes said. Before I could ask him more, Becky came through the door. I jumped to my feet, nearly tipping over what was left of our drinks.

"Mr. Holmes, may I present my fiancée, Miss Rebecca Louise Brower," I said proudly, just as Ma had taught me to do. "Becky, this is my good friend, Mr. Sherlock Holmes."

"Mr. Holmes, I'm delighted to meet you," Becky said. "I've heard so much about you."

"The pleasure is all mine," Holmes said pleasantly. I believe he meant it!

"I've reserved a table for us at the White House," I told them both.

"Ooh, fancy!" Becky cooed.

"It's only a few blocks away, on Fourth Street," I explained to Holmes, "but as cold as it's gotten, perhaps we should hail a cab."

The concert having been over for a while, we had no problem finding a hansom carriage to take us to the restaurant. On the way, Holmes and Becky had a chance to become familiar with one another. At first the conversation was polite, but a little stiff, as it can be between people meeting for the first time. That only lasted a few minutes, though. Before you knew it, we were all jabbering and laughing as if we'd known each other all our lives.

"I'm so happy you were able to join us," Holmes said to Becky, after we were seated in the huge banquet hall of the White House Restaurant.

"Well, I'm happy I could join you, too" Becky said. "It was tough to get away alone. All the girls in the group are just crazy about Lefty here."

"Why would they call you Lefty?" asked Holmes. "You write with your right hand, don't you? I've seen you throw snowballs that way, and shoot a gun, too."

"It's for the way I play the cornet," I explained. "Pa always fingered the valves with his left hand, because of the wounded tendons in his right wrist. So that's the way I started playing, too, and I've just stuck with it."

"Isn't it more difficult that way?" he asked.

"I don't know," I replied. "It's the only way I've tried. Besides, when I graduated school in Browns Valley, Muley gave me a cornet he'd reworked especially for me, with the bell tube winding around the right side of the valves, so I didn't have to cross over anymore. It not only improved my fingering, but something about the welding on the inside of the tube made it easier for me to play real high notes, without pinching or forcing them."

"Ooh, you should hear him play the high notes on that cornet of his," Becky chimed in. "He can even play the piccolo part on some of the new Sousa marches. It really gives their band a unique sound. It's one of the three reasons I fell in love with him, you know."

"Really," Holmes said, sounding amused. "And what are the other two, if I may ask?"

"His writing ability—and just his overall cuteness," she said, rumpling my hair.

"Stop it," I said half-heartedly (for I rather enjoyed it). "Everyone's looking."

In fact, everyone had been looking at Becky from the moment we walked into the room. She often attracted that kind of attention. She just stood out in a crowd—even a spiffy post-concert crowd like this, which, to say the least, was really quite elegant. The White House's claim to fame, besides first-class food, was its décor. Everything—the tables, the chairs, the piano, the sideboards, the bar, the draperies, the uniforms of the staff, you name it—was white. Ladies who wanted to draw attention to themselves regularly showed up in gaily colored dresses, or at least in black dresses with big, bright, bold sashes and hats. Not Becky. She had on a simple white dress, with just a hint of black brocade around the collar. Still, she was the most stunning woman in the room. She was going to be a beautiful bride!

Over dinner, our conversation turned to the wedding. Becky, of course, was all excited.

"It was my idea to get married the day after Christmas," she said. "I've always loved the way the church looks this time of year, with all the candles, the holly, the snow falling outside. And of course, the whole family will already be gathered together for the holidays, so the timing couldn't be better." There was another reason for the timing, too, I thought to myself; but no need to bring that up right now.

"It's supposed to be a small, family wedding," I explained. "But when you're talking about the Browers, the phrase 'small family' is a bit of an oxymoron."

"You and your fancy words," Becky teased me.

"You come from a large family, I take it?" Holmes asked her politely.

"Well," Becky replied slowly, "Father does have four brothers."

"And one of them has nine children!" I quickly piped in.

"I see," said Holmes, taken aback. "And will any of them be in the wedding party?"

"No," Becky laughed. "My brother Ripley—he's a lawyer—will be best man, and my sister Josephine—she's a schoolteacher—will be the maid of honor. That's it."

"What about your family, Peter?" Holmes asked.

"Well, Ma and Pa will be there, of course. Ma's brother, Dan, will be an usher, and his wife and kids will be there. Other than a couple of the boys from the band, that's it for my side—except for you, of course."

"Oh, yes, that reminds me of something," Becky said. "Peter, would you excuse us for a moment? I have a favor to ask of Mr. Holmes, and it's sort of a secret."

I consented, and walked over to stand at the bar for a while, watching them in the mirror. After a moment or two, I saw Holmes shake his head, responding negatively. I had no idea what she was asking him, but I knew Becks wouldn't give up that easily. She was both persistent and persuasive, and possessed a disarming charm that usually allowed her to get her way. Sure enough, before long they were laughing, nodding their heads in agreement, and motioning for me to come back to the table. The topic of their conversation, though, remained a secret.

By then, it was time for me to escort Becky back to her hotel. "Our chaperone will have a fit if I miss curfew," she told Holmes. "The college can be funny about that."

She explained that the Schubert Club was hosting a music workshop all day on Saturday, but she would be free to join me for ice skating at Aurora Park in the evening. Sunday, her group was heading back to St. Cloud. I said that Holmes and I planned to visit my new co-workers at the Dispatch on Saturday morning, and maybe trek over to the university in the afternoon.

"We'll probably join you on the train on Sunday," I said. "Then Mr. Holmes and I will head on to Browns Valley for a few days with my folks. We did some hunting the first time he was here. This time I'd like to take him ice fishing, if he's interested." Holmes nodded in affirmation. "Thursday, we'll take the train to Willmar, to spend Christmas Eve with Uncle Dan and his family. Christmas Day, we'll all pile into Dan's horse-drawn sleigh and head to St. Cloud, to join up with your family. Maybe we can make the horses look like reindeer, so your little cousins will think we're Santa Claus and his elves."

We all had a good laugh over that. Unfortunately, it was the last one we had for a while. Over the next few hours, all of our plans were about to change—to go up in smoke, you might say.

CHAPTER 8

THE FIRE

Becky's curfew was at 11. By midnight, I was back at the Grand Old Inn, sound asleep in my cozy bed. Some time later, I heard what sounded like the clanging bell of a fire engine. I paid it no mind. Later still, I heard a gentle tapping at my door. It turned out to be the overnight maid.

"Sorry to disturb you at this hour, sir," she said, when I cracked open the door. "The desk clerk sent me up. You have a visitor in the lobby."

"A visitor?" I asked, still half asleep. It must be Becky, I thought—which means there must be something wrong. "Man or woman?" I asked the maid.

"It's a man, sir," she said, "and I believe he has luggage."

"Give me a minute, I'll be right down," I told her. I had no idea who it could be. I certainly wasn't expecting anyone. When I got to the lobby, I was surprised to see Holmes.

"What's going on?" I asked him.

"There's been a fire," he explained. "They've evacuated the Ryan. They're transporting all the guests to other hotels. I came here."

"A fire?" I asked. "I guess I heard the fire engine earlier. What time is it?"

"Around three," he said. "The clerk said he has no more rooms, because of the holidays. Do you think you could possibly put me up for the night?"

"Of course," I said. "We'll take your bags right up. But tell me more about the fire. How bad is it? Was anyone injured?"

"No injuries that I know of," said Holmes, as we carried his bags up to the room. "They roused the hotel guests as soon as

46

flames began to spread from the Schutte Building. That's where the worst of it is, I hear."

"The Schutte Building?" I repeated. My heart skipped a beat.

"Yes," he said. "That's apparently where it started. We could see flames pouring out of the top three stories as we left. What's wrong? You look as if you just lost your best friend."

"The Superintendent," I stammered. "He sleeps there when he's in town. We have to get back down there right away, to see if he's alright!"

"I'm sorry, I didn't know," Holmes said. "Of course, I'll go with you. But I'm not sure they'll let us anywhere near the place. It was surrounded by firefighters and their equipment, and the police were keeping the public away."

"Well," I said, "I have to try. I want to be able to assure Becky that he's safe—IF he's safe."

As rapidly as I could, I threw on some warmer clothes, and we raced down to Seven Corners. The streetcars had long since shut down for the night, and all the cabs were busy carrying folks away from the fire, not toward it. Fortunately, we spotted Eisenmenger's meat wagon returning from its midnight bacon run to Fort Snelling, and were able to snag a ride.

When we reached Robert Street, the scene was just as Holmes had described it. The police had set up a blockade to keep gawkers away. To the east, Seventh Street was full of firefighters and their equipment. Hoses stretched in every direction, forming a tangled web amid the horse-drawn fire engines, tankers, pumpers and hook-and-ladder units. Obviously, more than the local brigade had been called into action.

The Schutte Building, all the way down to Jackson Street, was totally engulfed in flames, from top to bottom. Cardozo's Furniture Store was gutted. Firefighters appeared to be focusing their efforts on keeping the flames from leaping to the retail stores across the street. With everyone racing frantically about, shouting to be heard above the roar, it was obvious we would get no answers to our questions here.

We headed down Robert Street, to Sixth. Here, the fire looked to have been brought under control by the hoses. Icicles hung from stone ledges and window frames where the glass had been blown out, making large portions of the building look like a wintry mountain precipice. Though smoke still rose out of a few windows on the third and fourth floors, the Ryan Hotel had apparently been saved from extensive damage. In front of the Ryan, an assistant fire chief named Conlan was addressing the press.

"We won't know for sure until morning," he was saying, "but from the looks of things right now, the fire started in the back of the furniture store, at ground level."

"Then why were the upper floors of the building the first to burn?" someone asked.

"We think a draft pulled the fire up an elevator shaft, to the top floor, where it proceeded to burn its way back down," he explained. "By the time the fire department arrived, at two o'clock, we had flames on the bottom floor and the top two floors, working their way toward the middle."

That's where the Superintendent's office is, I thought.

"As we tried to force the fire away from that part of the building," Conlan continued, "it worked its way back toward the third and fourth floors of the Ryan Hotel. Fortunately, we were able to get everyone out of there in time, and additional volunteers from other brigades arrived to help bring that portion of the fire under control."

"What about the Schutte Building?" someone asked. "Are you going to be able to save it?"

Conlan paused to gather his words before he spoke. Finally, he answered. "The Schutte Building, I'm afraid, is almost a total loss. We're trying now to make sure the fire doesn't spread to any of the businesses on the other side of Seventh and Jackson Streets."

I couldn't stand it anymore. I had to ask. "Did you get everyone out of the Schutte Building?" I yelled above the crowd.

"I'm sorry, I'm only taking questions from the press," Conlan replied.

"Did you get everyone out of the Schutte Building?" someone else asked. I didn't know his name, but I recognized his face as someone from the Dispatch.

Conlan frowned. "As far as we know at this point, there were no fatalities, if that's what you're asking. Of course, we haven't been able to make a complete sweep of the building yet. We will accomplish that task as soon as possible, hopefully at daybreak. Any further questions?"

"Do you know the cause of the fire?" someone asked.

I didn't listen for the answer. I was too distraught about the possibility of Becky losing a father, for the second time. I turned to Holmes, but he was nowhere in sight. I was about to lose it, when Holmes emerged from the crowd, gripping another man by the elbow.

"Tell him what you told me," Holmes said to the man.

"Yeah, sure, I'm Nels Sandberg," the man said, in a thick Swedish accent. "I'm night watchman in the Schutte Building. I'm the one who called in the fire."

"Get to the point," Holmes urged him.

"Yeah, I woke up all the tenants on the third and fourth floors," the man said. "The rest of the building was empty."

"Mr. Brower, was he one of the tenants you woke?" I asked anxiously.

"You betcha," the watchman said. "The Superintendent, yeah, he was one of the first I went to. He wanted to box up a bunch of his belongings, but I told him, no, you get the heck out of here, as quick as you can. And he did."

"Thank you!" I said, with a sigh of relief. "Do you happen to know where he went?"

"To the Boardman," the man said, "to see his friend, Mr. Chaney."

"Thank you, thank you very much!" I said, shaking his hand.

"Feeling better now?" Holmes asked me, as Sandberg disappeared into the crowd.

"Absolutely!" I said. "Josiah Chaney is a longtime associate of J.V.'s, from the historical society. He keeps a room at the Boardman Hotel, on Ninth and Wabasha, near the state capitol. It's one of the first places Becky would look, when she gets word of the fire—if she can't reach me."

"Do you think we can get some sleep, then?" Holmes asked with a weary grin.

Despite the hour, we were able to catch a hansom cab back to the Grand Old Inn. Holmes insisted on taking the chair, and I collapsed on the bed. It was nearly 5:30 in the morning.

CHAPTER 9

BOOT PRINTS

Two hours later, we were back at the scene of the fire. After Holmes checked the body while Brower and I distracted Patrolman O'Harra, we went again to the White House Restaurant. To my surprise, their entire banquet hall had been turned into a house of respite for firefighters, utility workers and salvage crews, and a gathering place for refugees from the fire. It was the sort of charitable act you expected to see in a small town, but not the big city. I wondered how they would ever get the black soot off all the white furnishings. I wondered, too, how Holmes seemed to know so much about the killer. The Superintendent must have been wondering the same thing.

"How do you know his height and weight?" Brower asked Holmes, as soon as he had the chance.

"From his boot prints," Holmes said matter-of-factly.

"What boot prints?" I asked. "I didn't see any boot prints."

"Then you didn't look closely enough," Holmes told me. "They were there, two of them, on the basement floor, leading from the center of the storeroom to the door. That, Peter, is why I asked you to bring me a glass of water. And why I promptly poured it on the floor."

"I still don't understand," I said.

"The killer apparently stepped in a substance that was immiscible with water, probably the fuel he used to start the fire," Holmes explained. "Wherever he stepped on the floor, water from the fire hoses refused to mix with that substance, and formed into miniscule beads, several of which had frozen and were still visible to the naked eye when we arrived. Fortunately for us, when I poured more water on the floor, the globules gathered

50

in the shape of two very clear boot prints. The distance between the two boot prints, the man's stride, tells us that he is at least six feet tall. The wide dispersion of globules within each boot print tells us that he is fairly heavyset."

"I'll be darned," said the Superintendent. "And how do you know he's left-handed?"

"From the wound to the left front portion of the victim's skull," Holmes replied.

I thought about that for a moment, picturing the attack in my mind. "Wouldn't that make the killer right-handed?" I asked.

"Only if it were an overhand blow," Holmes said. "The angle of this wound indicates that it came from a sidearm blow. The victim's position in the corner of the room would have made it impossible for a right-handed man to deliver such a blow, without striking the adjoining wall. Therefore, it had to be a backhanded blow, by a left-handed man."

Brower then asked a delicate question. "Don't you think you should share this information with the police?"

"Oh, they'll figure it out soon enough, as soon as someone with more experience arrives on the scene," Holmes replied. "In the meantime, if young O'Harra's theory makes the newspapers, it may put our killer's mind at ease. If the killer becomes overconfident, he'll get careless. That will make him even easier to find—though finding him should be easy enough as it is."

"No disrespect, sir, but I don't know how you can say that," Brower offered. "There are nearly a hundred and sixty thousand people living in St. Paul. Probably a fourth of them are adult males. I have no idea how many are over six feet tall and heavyset, but it has to be thousands. Finding one man among that many, even a left-handed one, will be like finding a needle in a haystack."

"Ah, but I have two more clues," Holmes said. "Two clues that will tell me what kind of work he does, and approximately where he lives." With that, he pulled a kerchief out of his coat. When he spread it out on the table, we could see the impression of a boot print.

"In England," Holmes explained, "every boot carries the markings of its maker. It might be a distinctive pattern in the sole, something special about the stitching, a tiny insignia near the toe or heel, but always something to distinguish one manufacturer's work from another's.

"It's likely the same here in America," he went on. "I'm certain that if I visit a couple of those boot manufacturers that Peter and I walked past yesterday, I can find out not only where the boot was made, but also where it might have been sold. Since people tend to shop close to home, if I can find the neighborhood in which this boot was purchased, I'll have a better idea of where the man who purchased it lives."

"How will you find out where he works?" I asked.

"The type of boot itself will tell us something about his occupation," Holmes said. "Beyond that, we have traces of the liquid in which he stepped—the fuel he used to start the fire. If, as it appears, he brought it with him to the scene, chances are he obtained it where he works."

"Again," Brower objected, "it could be any of hundreds of places."

"I don't think so," Holmes replied. "As I mentioned, the substance has a kerosene-like smell, but it feels much thicker, with a heavier texture. It's actually quite unique. If I can procure a Bunsen burner and a few vials, I can ascertain its exact chemical composition. That will tell us in which industry it is commonly employed. If we can find the source of the fuel, we'll find our killer."

"You might be able to get a Bunsen burner at the Emporium," Brower suggested. "They stock a wide variety of useful gadgets."

"St. Paul Book and Stationery has a contract to provide school and university supplies," I added. "They might have something like that as well."

"I'd better get at it then" Holmes said, rising from his seat. "I have a few other items I need to procure as well, but I think I know where to find them. Peter, will you be joining me?"

"Actually," Brower said, "I was hoping Peter might be able to help me today, and tomorrow as well. They promised to let me go through my storeroom as soon as the chief of detectives has examined and removed the body. Tomorrow, if the fire chief decides it's structurally safe, they may let me check my third-floor office as well. I'd like to prepare a complete inventory of everything that was lost, to file with my insurance agent on Monday morning."

I would rather have gone with Holmes, but agreed to stay with the Superintendent, at least until my date with Becky that evening.

"That's totally understandable," Holmes said. I'm sure he saw the disappointment on my face, though I did my best to hide it from Brower.

"Superintendent," Holmes said, shaking his hand, "I'm sorry for your loss. I hope it turns out to be not as bad as it might appear. And Peter, I'll catch up with you sometime later today, back at the Grand. I suspect it will be another day before they'll let me move back into the Ryan."

I did not see Holmes again that afternoon, or in the early part of the evening. After several hours of sorting through the rubble and ashes of the Superintendent's basement storeroom, I returned to the Grand Old Inn for a long, hot bath. Refreshed, I then met Becky, and we headed for Aurora Park.

The park was located at the corner of Dale Street North and Aurora Avenue, one block south of the intercity streetcar line that linked St. Paul and Minneapolis via University Avenue. For the past two summers, the area had been dubbed Comiskey Park, after the former St. Louis Browns and Cincinnati Reds first-sacker who now owned the St. Paul Saints Base Ball Club.

In his team's first two seasons at Dale and Aurora, Comiskey had run into one problem after another. First, thousands of fans discovered that they could avoid the half-dollar admission fee by watching the game from a huge hill across St. Albans Street, which flanked one side of the stadium. Comiskey solved this problem by building a tall set of bleachers to block their view. Fans had to climb a ladder to reach the seats, which were so high off the ground they became known as the nosebleed section.

Next, Comiskey discovered that neighborhood youngsters had drilled more than two hundred peepholes in the wooden outfield fence. He foiled the knothole gang by erecting a second wooden fence, half a foot inside the first one.

His third challenge was more problematic. Religious zealots along Dale Street had forbidden the Saints to play games on Sunday. After two years of haggling, residents said they might occasionally allow the rare game to be played on a Sunday—if it coincided with the city Fourth of July Celebration, for example—but in no way, shape or form would Comiskey ever be allowed to sell beer on the Sabbath. That was the final straw. In four months, the St. Paul Saints were scheduled to open their 1897 season in a new ball park, one mile to the west. Apparently, residents in the Lexington Avenue neighborhood weren't nearly so strict.

To help cover the cost of the new stadium, Comiskey had flooded the grounds at Dale and Aurora, and was hosting several events associated with the annual winter carnival. On this evening, in addition to open skating for the public, there were sponsored races, a polo match, and a brass band. Despite the cold, a large, festive crowd had turned out. Though most of the night's activities were outdoors, there was a huge tent at one end of the rink, with a couple of pot-bellied stoves to warm you up. Here, vendors sold hot chocolate, giant cinnamon sticks and various other goodies. On one of our trips to the warming area, Becky and I were approached by a scruffy, old vagrant.

"Spare a penny, to help an old man warm his innards?" he asked, holding out a hand. His bare fingers stuck through his ragged glove. His coat was tattered as well, and an ill-fitting homburg nearly covered his eyes. His scraggly beard looked like a robin's nest.

"Here," I said, giving him a nickel, "Merry Christmas. Don't spend it all on wine."

"In fact, Peter, that's exactly what I intend to do," he said. I did a double-take.

"What's the matter?" he asked. "Don't you recognize your own roommate?"

It was Holmes!

"What the devil are you doing in that getup?" I asked him. "And where on Earth did you get it?"

"I got it from the prop department at one of the local theaters," he said. "I thought I'd test it out on you, before going down to the levee."

"I'd say you passed the test, definitely," I told him. "What's going on at the levee?"

"I hear the hobos gather around a campfire under the railroad bridge," he explained. "I thought if I posed as one of them, and brought along a cheap bottle of wine, I might be able to learn a thing or two about our victim."

"Well, good luck with that," I told him. "How'd you make out with the boot print?"

"No luck at all," he replied. "I called on nearly a dozen boot manufacturers, wholesalers and retailers. Every one told me the same thing: There is nothing distinctive about the boot print. It is from the most common and inexpensive boot made. Every manufacturer makes it, and because it's the bottom-of-the-line model, nobody bothers to put their mark on it. Hundreds have been sold, from dozens of stores. All I learned is that it's made for laborers who are on their feet all day. Our killer could be someone who works in a factory, or a warehouse, on a loading dock, as a night watchman—or even a foot patrolman. We've narrowed the field very little, I'm afraid."

"Maybe you'll have better luck identifying the substance on the boot," suggested Becky, who had heard the whole story from me that evening. "Were you able to find a Bunsen burner?"

"Yes, I found everything I needed," Holmes told her. Then, turning to me, he added, "and if you don't mind, Peter, I'd like to set it up in a corner of our room tonight, after I get back from the levee. Will it bother you if I work quietly, while you sleep?"

"Not a bit," I said. "After the night we had last night, and the way Ol'Man Rivers worked me this afternoon, followed by ice skating tonight, I think I can sleep through anything."

CHAPTER 10

THE BULL

I was right. I slept like a baby. I did not hear Holmes return from the levee. I did wake up once during the night, to use the bathroom. Holmes was in a corner of the hotel room, working with his vials and Bunsen burner. He did not appear to notice me, and I didn't speak to him. Hours later, he woke me from my slumber again, just as he had the morning before.

"Peter, wake up," he said. "The desk clerk came with a message from the Superintendent. He wants to see us right away, at police headquarters. Rather, I should say, the chief of detectives wants to see us. It sounded rather urgent."

I scrambled to my feet and got dressed as quickly as I could. From what I'd heard of John J. O'Connor, if he requested your presence, you'd better not be late. They called him the Big Fellow, but it was more for the power he wielded than for his physical stature. They also called him the Bull, for the way he liked to throw his weight around. He'd been on the police force fifteen years, and had already worked his way up to chief of detectives. Rumor was he had his eye on the job of chief of the entire police department, and God help anybody who got in his way.

Brower was already with the chief of detectives when we arrived. After the Superintendent made the introductions, O'Connor got right to the point.

"Mr. Holmes," he said, "we were just discussing a few discrepancies in Patrolman O'Harra's theory about the dead body that was found in Superintendent Brower's storeroom. Perhaps you'd like to help us clear them up?"

"I'll be happy to do what I can," Holmes said. "But first, Chief, may I ask you a question?"

"Go ahead," said O'Connor, with some reluctance.

"Are you familiar," Holmes asked, "with a former prizefighter named Klaus Mueller?"

O'Connor paused for a long moment, then finally answered. "Yes, I may have heard of him. I believe they called him Mueller the Mauler, if I'm not mistaken."

"Would you mind telling me why you've hired him to follow me?" Holmes asked.

"Why, I've done no such thing!" the chief protested.

"Come now, sir, we are both professionals," Holmes countered. "Can we not discuss this in an open, mature manner?"

Again the chief paused, then confessed. "OK, you've caught me. Yes, I hired Mueller to tail you. I heard you were going to be here, and I wanted to know what you were up to."

"All I am up to," Holmes replied, "is to help my good friend, Mr. Brower, clear up this matter as quickly as possible, so he can enjoy his daughter's wedding at the end of the week."

"I see," O'Connor said, glancing at Brower, who'd been uncommonly quiet during this entire exchange. "Unfortunately, Mr. Holmes, your reputation precedes you. You are well known for showing up the local constabulary wherever you go. I merely wanted to ensure that, if I couldn't stay one step ahead of you, I'd at least be no more than one step behind you. I apologize for my actions, and for my little fib a moment ago."

"I assure you, sir, I have no intention of showing you up, as you say," Holmes replied. "Now that we have come to an understanding, I shall keep you abreast of my progress, you have my word."

"Thank you for your indulgence, I truly appreciate it," O'Connor said. "What about the tail, shall I call him off?"

Holmes shook his head. "No, Herr Mueller may eventually be of some use," he suggested. "Just let him know that he must in no way hinder me. And if I should ever request his assistance, he must act without a moment's hesitation."

"Consider it done, sir," O'Connor agreed. "Now, moving on to the matter of the dead body in Superintendent Brower's storeroom: Contrary to Patrolman O'Harra's theory, I have reason to believe there was a second man involved. Do you concur?"

"I do," Holmes replied, nodding.

"I also believe this second man is guilty of killing the first man, do you agree?"

"I do," Holmes said again.

The Bull appeared to be losing patience. "Do you have any other notions about the second man?" he asked brusquely, again glancing at Brower, though I wasn't sure why.

"I do," Holmes said once more, apparently enjoying this little game. Then, to my surprise, he told the chief of detectives all about the boot prints he'd discovered. He also explained how the boot prints allowed him to estimate the killer's height and weight. And, finally, how the victim's wound indicated a backhanded blow from a left-handed man.

"Yes, yes, we're aware of all that," O'Connor said smugly. I wasn't sure if he was telling the truth or not. He had been writing down everything Holmes said. "And I'm sure you are aware, Mr. Holmes, that you have just described Superintendent Brower?"

For the moment, Holmes was speechless. I was flabbergasted! Brower was the first to speak.

"I'm right-handed," he protested. "Besides, why would I set fire to my life's work?"

"To cover up a murder," the Bull shot back.

"And why would I commit a murder?" Brower asked.

"You tell me," O'Connor suggested.

"Now see here," Holmes said to the chief of detectives, "I object to this line of questioning. Surely you don't suspect Mr. Brower of this crime!"

"Mr. Holmes," O'Connor said, "before you arrived, we already established the fact that the Superintendent has no alibi for the time of the murder. He returned from a meeting before ten-thirty, went to his office alone, and wasn't seen again until Nels Sandberg roused him sometime after two o'clock in the morning. That gave him a four-hour window of opportunity."

"I see," Holmes said. "And what was his motive?"

"That's what I'm trying to find out," O'Connor replied. "Surely you understand: At the moment, I have no suspects, so I must suspect everyone."

"Then I assume," said Holmes, "that I am a suspect too, along with Peter here as well?"

"Of course not," O'Connor replied.

"And why not?" Holmes asked. Again, they were playing a game of cat and mouse.

"The answer is very simple, Mr. Holmes," the Bull said confidently. "Herr Mueller has already accounted for your presence at every moment on the night of the murder. The desk clerk at the Grand can vouch for young Mr. Smith's whereabouts after he left you. Mr. Brower enjoys no such luxury."

As Holmes again objected that O'Connor was barking up the wrong tree, the Bull shook him off.

"Mr. Brower," O'Connor said, though his eyes were on Holmes, "since you appear to have no alibi, I accused you of the murder in order to gauge your reaction, which I've dutifully noted. I'm certain Mr. Holmes will agree that I was only doing what is required of me in such a situation. Personally, I would be very much surprised if you were guilty of such a crime. Professionally, however, I must continue to regard you as a suspect, until evidence tells me otherwise."

O'Connor had deftly recovered from the defensive position that Holmes had put him in at the start of this conversation. He clearly enjoyed being on the attack, and in control. It was easy to see why they called him the Bull.

"Now that we have that out of the way," the Bull continued, "we can proceed in a more logical direction. Mr. Holmes, has your taking of the boot print allowed you to make any progress?"

Holmes admitted that searching for the source of the boot had led to a dead end.

"Ah, then you're no farther along than we are," O'Connor said. He sounded relieved.

"Perhaps not," Holmes acknowledged. "But I do have one other lead." He then told all of us about his chemical analysis of the substance the killer had tracked across the floor.

"Chemically speaking, it's a liquid hydrocarbon," Holmes said. "In more practical terms, it is a combustible petroleum distillate, similar to kerosene, only much heavier. About five years ago, an Englishman named Herbert Akroyd Stuart used such a substance to fuel the world's first compression-ignition oil engine."

"What does that have to do with anything in St. Paul?" O'Connor asked.

"A good question," Holmes acknowledged. "To my knowledge, Stuart never found a market for his invention. But I understand that a French scientist named Diesel, working in Germany, has filed a patent for an engine—using a similar fuel—that he believes could power a locomotive. With more than two hundred trains passing through your city every day, I'm wondering if any of them might be using such a fuel."

"I have no idea," O'Connor said. "But I know someone who would."

"James J. Hill!" Brower and I said simultaneously.

"Exactly," the chief of detectives said. "He's been known to work on Sunday. If you gentlemen will excuse me for a moment, I'll give his office a call to see if he might be available."

While the chief of detectives was gone, Holmes turned to me.

"Peter, about your plans for the next couple of days, . . ." I already knew what was coming. "We may have to delay our trip to Browns Valley for a day or two, if you don't mind? Of course, you could always go by yourself."

"Oh, no, I'm sticking with you," I said. "I'm sure my folks will understand."

By then, Chief of Detectives O'Connor had returned.

"Mr. Hill is down with some seasonal ailment," the Bull said. "He's agreed to see you at his home at three o'clock this afternoon. Unfortunately, I won't be able to join you. But I'm sure you'll let me know what you find out?"

"Of course," Holmes replied, "you have my word on that."

"Good," O'Connor said. "Now, before you leave, I have one or two more questions for the Superintendent. Sir, do you have any enemies?"

Brower seemed relieved by this turn in the questioning. He began to laugh. "In my search for the truth," he replied, "I'm afraid I may have stepped on the toes of any number of men—from James Gordon Bennett, Jr. to President Thomas Jefferson, were he still alive."

"Why do you ask?" Holmes wanted to know.

"My suspicion," the Bull continued, "is that our perpetrator was out to steal or destroy something in Mr. Brower's possession, for whatever reason, and the victim just happened to get in the way—in the wrong place at the wrong time, you might say."

"Interesting," Holmes mused.

"Do you have another theory?" O'Connor asked.

"Based on the viciousness of the blow," Holmes said, "I believe that the killer knew the victim. He tracked him to the Schutte Building, intending to confront him, perhaps even to kill him. It is just by coincidence that it happened in the Superintendent's storeroom."

"Well, we shall see who is right, then," the Bull said. It sounded like a challenge. "At the moment, none of us knows much about the killer, or the victim, for that matter."

"I beg to differ," Holmes said. "The victim's name is Padraig Doherty. He worked as a type compositor for the Fargo Forum for the past twenty years. He was fired when he turned to drink after losing his leg in a piece of machinery, and came to St. Paul looking for work."

"How the devil do you know that?" O'Connor blurted. He was obviously surprised.

"I learned it from the hobos, under the railroad bridge at the levee," Holmes said.

"We rousted them all last night!" the Bull argued. "I personally spoke with half a dozen of them. None of them knew a thing!"

"None of them knew anything they were willing to tell you, Chief," Holmes said. "They might have told you something, if you'd treated them a little more kindly. In fact, I might have told you the man's name last night myself, if you hadn't treated me so rudely."

"Last night?" O'Connor asked. "You were there?"

"Indeed I was, guv'nor," Holmes said, faking an old man's accent. Then, as we rose to leave, Holmes had these parting words: "Remember, Chief: a bottle of cheap wine and a bit of kindness will harvest a lot more information than a bully with a billy club."

The look on Bull O'Connor's face when we left was the same as the one on Herr Mueller's face, the night he held the door open for us at Magee's.

CHAPTER 11

MURDER WEAPON

As we left the police station, Holmes said he had suddenly grown weary. I wasn't surprised. He'd been up nearly all night, two nights in a row. He went back to the Grand to take a nap.

Meanwhile, the Superintendent and I returned to the Schutte Building. Chief O'Connor had arranged for us to gain access to the third floor. Around a late-morning break to see Becky off at the train station, we gave Mr. Brower's office the same going-over we'd given his storeroom the day before. When Holmes joined us mid-afternoon, we had startling news for him.

"I think we've found the murder weapon," I announced.

"Actually, we haven't found it, we've discovered it missing," Brower corrected me.

"What is it?" Holmes asked.

"A sword!" I replied. I couldn't hide my excitement.

"I'm sorry," Holmes said, shaking his head. "A sword would have made a cleaner and much deeper wound than the one I saw."

"What if it were in a scabbard?" I asked.

"What kind of a scabbard?" he wanted to know. I looked at Brower.

"A metal scabbard," he said, "made of nickeled steel, I believe."

"Smooth?" Holmes asked.

"Mostly," Brower replied.

"That would account for the depth of the wound. But the edges were jagged," Holmes said.

"The scabbard had three metal bands, with ornate relief images on them," Brower said.

"Where?" Holmes asked, growing more interested.

"One at the top, with a frog stud and two suspension rings, to attach it to a belt; one at the bottom, to protect the tip; and one in the middle, for . . . decoration."

"How long was the middle band, the decorative one?" Holmes asked.

"Three, maybe four inches," Brower replied.

"That's it!" Holmes said. "Gentlemen, I believe you're right, we have a murder weapon. Now all we have to do is find it! Can you describe the sword, please?"

"It has a straight, double-edged blade, about thirty inches long, maybe three-quarters of an inch wide. My name, J. V. Brower, is etched on one side, flanked by foliate scrolls. The grip is ivory. It also has my initials, J. V. B., on one side. The back sides of both the sword and the grip have . . . decorative etchings."

"Of a knight in armor, and a banner bearing a cross," Holmes offered.

"That's right," Brower said. "How did you know?"

"It's the Knight Templar sword," Holmes replied. "Come now, sir, this is not the first time I've run across a member of the Freemasons. We do have them in Europe as well, you know! I admire their dedication and service, and congratulate you on achieving such an honor. I do not understand the society's desire for secrecy, but I will respect it. Now, where was the sword kept?"

"Usually in a large drawer, in my office," Brower said. "But a month or two ago, I needed to make room for other things, so I moved the sword down to the storeroom for safekeeping, or so I thought. I guess I'd forgotten I moved it, which is why I didn't miss it yesterday. It was on a shelf, in plain view. I thought it was safe, since I had the only key to the locked door."

"Well, when we find the killer, we potentially will have one more piece of evidence to link him to the crime," Holmes said. "Now, we'd better go see this Mr. Hill of yours, to find out if he can tell us the source of the mysterious fuel."

Mr. James Jerome Hill was known across America as the Empire Builder. His pet project, the Great Northern Railway, played a major role in the expansion of the American Northwest, in terms of settlement, commerce and agriculture. He was one of the most powerful men in St. Paul, as well as one of the richest.

He and his family lived in a huge stone mansion on Summit Avenue, atop Selby Hill, overlooking the west side of lowertown St. Paul.

To get there, we hopped on a streetcar at Robert Street and headed west on Seventh. As we rode, Holmes said he was curious about Bull O'Connor's comment, about his "reputation" preceding him.

"He's probably read some of Dr. Watson's stories," I suggested.

Holmes looked surprised. "I knew Watson's publisher had shipped copies of his books to New York," Holmes said. "I never imagined they'd reach this part of the country."

"Oh, yes, A Study in Scarlet was very popular here," Brower offered. "All of my friends have read it."

"I can't imagine why," Holmes said drily.

"Probably because folks hereabout can all relate to the characters in the story," Brower explained. "A large number of Minnesotans, myself included, still have relatives back in Indiana and Ohio. If my memory serves me correctly, that part of the country was home to the perpetrator, Jefferson Hope, as well as both victims, Stangerson and Drebber."

"Humph," Holmes grunted. "And Peter has read The Sign of the Four, though not very closely, I'm afraid."

I ignored the gibe. "I've also read some of Watson's short stories that have been published in The Strand," I said, referring to the popular magazine. "Ma always lets me know when a new one arrives at the library. My favorite case is The Speckled Band."

"My wife and daughters loved A Scandal in Bohemia," Brower said. "They're all intrigued by the woman, Irene Adler."

Suddenly, Holmes looked embarrassed. He did not have a comeback for that one. Fortunately for him, our streetcar had reached West Third Street, where we were required to disembark and transfer to the Selby Avenue line. At the bottom of Selby Hill, we stopped momentarily.

"What's going on?" Holmes asked.

"The grade is too steep for the electric cars," Brower explained. "We're hooking up to a cable car, to pull us up the hill. On the way back, we'll use the cable car as a counterweight, or drag, to help us brake down the hill. They do the same thing to get up and down Dayton's Bluff, on the east side of town."

"Amazing," Holmes said. "Why don't they just stick with cable cars all over?"

"They don't work well in the winter," Brower explained. "When the slots for the cable and the rails aren't filling up with ice and snow, they're expanding or contracting because of the extreme cold. It causes all kinds of problems. When it got too expensive to run horse-drawn streetcars, they tried steam-powered cars for a while. People complained about the noise and soot. The city switched over to electrified cars about three years ago, but you still see a cable car here and there, and even a few horse cars on some of the outlying lines."

"And the operators of all these different lines, they all get along?" Holmes asked.

"Actually," I replied, "there's only one operator, Mr. Thomas Lowry. His Twin City Rapid Transit Company owns all of the streetcar lines in St. Paul, and Minneapolis as well. He also runs a line between the two cities, along University Avenue. He's even talking about building a line out to Excelsior, on Lake Minnetonka."

"You don't say," Holmes replied indifferently. Then, he changed the subject.

"Peter," he said, "do you mind if I make a suggestion?"

"Not at all," I answered. I had no idea what was coming.

"On our last case together," he began, "it was I who operated incognito. This time around, I think it is your turn to do so."

"OK," I said, not quite sure what he meant. "Would you mind telling me why?"

"In my experience," he said, "if people know there's a newspaper reporter present, they do one of two things. Either they exaggerate, in hopes of looking better in the eyes of the public. Or they clam up, in fear of looking bad. Either way, it distorts the truth. I doubt if someone as experienced as your Mr. Hill will be affected, but it's likely he's not the only one we'll be interviewing. It might be better, at least for the next day or two, if you claim to be a recent graduate from the school of business, rather than journalism. Do you mind?"

"Not at all," I said again. "It sounds like fun!"

By now we'd reached the summit of Selby Hill. I could see the Hill Mansion looming a short distance away. It was time to meet the Empire Builder.

CHAPTER 12

EMPIRE BUILDERS

When we reached 240 Summit Avenue, we walked through the wrought iron gate, up the paved, curved driveway, under the red sandstone arches of the carriage porch, and toward the big mahogany front doors of the Hill Mansion. A servant must have been watching for us, as the door opened immediately, and we were directed into a small reception room to our left. It was filled with black and white photographs—round, red-tinted photos of children: children sledding and skating, children on horseback, children climbing trees, children picking apples, children making jam, children riding wagons, children fishing, you name it. We barely had time to admire a few of them, before an attractive young lady entered the room.

"Papa will see you now," she said. We left the reception room and entered a long, wide hallway, centered by a huge wooden staircase. A short distance to the left, we were led into the drawing room, where the great James Jerome Hill stood up to greet us as Mr. Brower made the introductions.

"I imagine the Superintendent here has filled your head will all sorts of nonsense about rivers?" Hill immediately asked Holmes.

"Ah, you know me too well, sir," Brower said good-naturedly. Holmes merely smiled as he shook the railroad magnate's hand.

"Well, don't you believe a word of it," Hill continued. "It's the railroad that made this country what it is today! In Minnesota alone, there are more than forty thousand miles of railroad track. Think of where this state would be without them."

"There are ninety thousand miles of rivers in Minnesota," Brower countered.

"And not a one of them is navigable more than seven months of the year!" Hill replied. As he gestured for us to sit, our host noted that railroads had hauled ninety-two million bushels of Minnesota-raised grain to market this year, plus twelve and a half million barrels of flour, a hundred and fifty million pounds of fruit, I forget how many tons of livestock, and nearly six hundred million board-feet of lumber. "That's eleven million dollars worth of wood!" he exclaimed. "Why, this state would still be nothing but a desolate territory, were it not for the railroad, I'm telling you straight."

"This coming from a man who made his fortune—his first fortune, mind you—in the steamboat business," Brower interjected.

"I've made my living in the transportation business," Hill replied, "transporting goods, and people, to where they needed to be. It's what made this state grow, from practically nothing, to what it is today."

It was fun to hear the two men banter. Few men would dare talk that way to Brower; fewer still to Hill! The two had been friends for many years, at least since the early 1880s, when Hill was pushing his railroad westward to compete with the Northern Pacific. Brower had helped him acquire the right-of-way to several key tracts of land in Todd County, as well as thousands of acres of oak trees, to be used for railroad ties and bridge timbers. In return, Hill made sure the newly platted town of Browerville was one of the stops on what became known as the K-Line, heading north from Sauk Centre.

As a maid served coffee and tea, our host took another tack. "Mr. Holmes," Hill said, "I understand you've ridden the rails, from St. Paul to Dakota?"

"I have," Holmes confirmed, "though it was ten years ago now."

"Perfect!" Hill said. "Now, on your journey, did you happen to notice that a big, wooden grain elevator seemed to pop up every seven miles or so?"

"As a matter of fact, I did," Holmes replied.

"That's because," Hill explained, "when that stretch of rail was laid, seven miles was as far as a steam locomotive could go before its water boiler needed to be refilled. So wherever you see a grain elevator built, you can bet the railroad had a water tank there first."

"And right behind the water tank and grain terminal, there came a saloon," Brower joked.

Hill chuckled. "We prefer to call it a grocery, but you see my point," he said. "The railroad is responsible for starting and maintaining hundreds of towns along its tracks."

"And every one of them near a river or a stream," Brower added.

"Ah, you never give up, do you?" Hill said, shaking his head.

Brower took advantage of the opening. "You'll notice that our host hasn't mentioned the mining industry in northern Minnesota," Brower pointed out. "That's because it's Jay Cooke's railroad, not James J. Hill's, that hauls iron ore to the harbor in Duluth."

"I should have known, one Dutchman sticking up for another," Hill replied. "Cooke's railroad has only served to make richer men out of ship builders in Cleveland, steel makers in Pittsburgh, and coal miners in Kentucky. It's done nothing for the good folks of St. Paul."

"It's still more than you'll be able to do, once Debs and his group down at 309 Wabasha get done with you," Brower said amiably. The address cited was the site of Assembly Hall, headquarters of the American Railway Workers Union. Eugene Debs was their fiery president.

"We dealt with the Grange," Hill shrugged. "We'll deal with the unions."

"Excuse me, what is the Grange?" Holmes asked.

"A group of farmers who tried to wrest control from the railroads by building their own grain elevators," Brower explained.

"And how did you deal with that?" Holmes asked Hill.

"Supply and demand, my good man, supply and demand," Hill replied. "Whenever a farmer delivered grain to one of our elevators, we made sure we had a stack of cord wood or a bin of coal out front, so he didn't have to go home with an empty wagon."

I felt it was time for me to get involved in the conversation. "Why didn't you just offer them a higher price?" I asked, to my immediate regret.

"Good Lord, young man, have they taught you nothing at that school of yours?" bellowed Hill. "There are a dozen things wrong with that notion, but I'll give you just two. First, it should be obvious, that would cost us more—and the number one key to staying in business is to keep your costs down. Second, it would have strengthened the Grange's fight to get the government to step in and regulate things. And the more the government gets involved in something, the bigger a mess you've got, you can take my word on that!"

"Well, gentlemen," Holmes said, coming to my rescue, "before we sink into a discussion of politics, I do have a specific question about railroads." Holmes then told about the fuel he'd analyzed, and asked Hill if he'd ever heard of Stuart or Diesel.

"Oh, I've heard of Diesel, alright," Hill said. "But he's not ready to power a locomotive yet. Believe me, I'd be the first to know."

"He's right about that," Brower agreed. "James was among the first to foresee the railroads' switch from wood to coal as a fuel. Of course, this was after he'd purchased the rights to the largest coal deposit in Iowa—which is where he made his second fortune."

Hill just smiled and shook his head.

"I've also heard the same fuel system could be used for refrigeration, do you know anything about that?" Holmes asked Hill.

"All of our reefers are owned by Armour," Hill said, referring to refrigerated railroad cars belonging to the big meat-packing company. "I happen to know they still use ice to keep meat cold, that and a sophisticated combination of insulation and ventilation. But now that you mention it, I have heard that some of the local beer brewers are switching to mechanical refrigeration. If you'd like, I'll have my man, Stephens, get you a meeting with Theodore Hamm first thing tomorrow morning. I'll even have my driver pick you up in my carriage to take you there. Where are you staying?"

As we were discussing the arrangements for Monday morning, the attractive young lady came back into the room. "Papa," she said, "you need to get your rest before dinner."

Hill tried to wave her off. "I'm sorry, gentlemen," she said to the rest of us. "He does this every year just before Christmas—works himself into a fever, because he knows he has to take a few days off for the holidays."

"Now, Tolly, these men don't need to hear about my medical history," Hill replied. Then, to the rest of us, "But Clara Anne is right. I do need to get ready for dinner. I'd invite you all to join us, but the Archbishop is coming, and believe me, you don't want to get caught up in the middle of that conversation!"

As we got up to leave, Holmes asked Hill about the photos in the reception room. "Yes, our daughter, Charlotte, is quite the little Niepce," Hill said. "She helped put Eastman Kodak on the map, I'm afraid."

We were taking a different route back to the front door. As we passed through what I later learned was the Music room, we saw six more photos atop a piano. Unlike the candid family shots we had seen in the reception room, these appeared to be professionally made portraits.

"Are those your daughters?" Holmes asked Hill.

"Yes, all six of them," Hill said, assigning names to each of the images. "We lost a seventh, little Katie, in infancy."

"I'm sorry for your loss," Holmes said. "You have only girls, then?"

"Oh, no," Hill laughed. "James and Louis were off at Yale when these pictures were made. Young Walter didn't want to be grouped with the girls, so we keep his picture elsewhere."

With that, we said our goodbyes, and headed out into the snow. On our way down Selby Hill, Holmes asked Brower about the Archbishop.

"Archbishop John Ireland," Brower explained, "is something of an empire builder himself. Over the past thirty-five years, he's brought thousands of Irish immigrants to Minnesota, establishing dozens of Roman Catholic colonies all across the western prairies."

Brower explained that Hill and Ireland had known each other for decades, since Hill's wife, Mary, had grown up with the Ireland children. The two men had worked in cahoots for many years, alternating in the roles of land agent and banker, as Ireland founded colony after colony along Hill's railroad line. In recent times, though, they'd had a bit of a falling out.

"Why is that?" Holmes wanted to know.

"For one thing," Brower explained, "they disagree on the role of labor unions. Worse than that, I think, was Ireland's involvement in real estate dealings in the St. Thomas area with Thomas Lowry."

"The streetcar man?" Holmes asked.

"One and the same," Brower replied. "A few years back, Lowry joined a group, led by a man named W. D. Washburn, in financing the Sault Ste. Marie Railway. The Soo Line, as it was known, allowed the flour millers in Minneapolis to bypass Hill's Eastern Line, and ship their products directly to Duluth. For years, Hill had been charging Minneapolis higher rates than he charged St. Paul, and it ended up costing him millions of dollars. He's not yet forgiven Lowry for that, nor Ireland, by association."

"I see," said Holmes. "I was just wondering about the Archbishop, because that was the second time I've heard his name this weekend."

It was not to be the last.

CHAPTER 13

BEER BARONS

Hill's carriage picked us up bright and early the next morning. A Negro named Emerson Lewis was at the reins. Holmes and I were his only passengers. Brower had to meet with his insurance agent, then report back to police headquarters. It seems Bull O'Connor had not finished questioning him before we'd left so abruptly the previous morning. I suspect the chief of detectives also wanted a report on Holmes' progress.

As promised, Hill had arranged for us to meet with Theodore Hamm, proprietor of the largest and most modern brewery in St. Paul. Hamm immigrated to Minnesota from Germany in the 1850s. For years, he and his wife, Louise, operated a saloon and boarding house near Seven Corners. In the early 1860s, Hamm loaned money to a boarder named Andrew Keller, who owned a small local brewery. When Keller couldn't repay the debt, Hamm took over the man's business. Known then as the Excelsior Brewery, it was located at the corner of Greenbrier and Minnehaha streets, on the east shore of Phalen Creek, atop Dayton's Bluff.

When Hamm assumed control of the brewery, in 1864, it was producing five hundred barrels a year. Within fifteen years, Hamm was producing nearly fifty times that. Within twenty-five years, production capacity had increased by more than a hundredfold. Another major expansion of the facilities had begun in 1893. By the turn of the century, it was said, Theodore Hamm Brewing Company would be shipping half a million barrels of beer a year.

When Keller owned the company, he'd been able to deliver the brewery's daily output himself by wheelbarrow. By 1896,

Hamm had a stable of more than ninety Percherons to pull his horse-drawn delivery wagons. Many of those deliveries were to Union Depot, where Hill's railroad shipped Hamm's beer to the Dakotas and beyond. Despite this seemingly cozy business relationship, the beer baron had little good to say about the railroad magnate. As it turned out, the main thing Hamm had against Hill, other than his shipping rates, appeared to be the fact that the latter wasn't German.

"The Irish and the Swedes," Theodore Hamm told us, in a heavy German accent, "all came to America to escape something: famine, poverty, probably even jail for some of them. The Germans, now, we came to America looking for opportunity. We were businessmen, craftsmen, shopkeepers, artists. We came to Minnesota prepared, with skills, with experience, with capital! The Irishmen who came to Minnesota were dirt farmers or common laborers, and they came without a pot, if you know what I mean."

"I believe I've heard the expression," Holmes said. Like me, he had to be impressed by the man's overwhelming pride in his native country, after more than forty years in this one.

"And now look at them," Hamm went on. "Thanks to James J. Hill and his like, the Irish have risen to positions of management in the railroad, and all the firms that do business with them. Not to mention the way they've taken over the city: cops, firemen, aldermen, city clerks. No wonder the Irish always get the best contracts! Why, now I've heard that the Butler Brothers have the inside track on the new state capitol building. It never ends!"

He must have a relative, another German, in the construction business, I thought to myself. Fortunately, Holmes brought his rant to an end by asking about mechanical refrigeration.

"Don't use it, don't need to," Hamm declared. "We've got Lake Phalen right behind us, source of the cleanest ice in the world. And we've got the caves beneath us."

I'd heard about the caves. They were quite common in the limestone bluffs that lined this part of the Mississippi River. They'd served all manner of purposes over the years, some legal and some not. For decades, brewers had used the huge network of cool underground caverns to store and age thousands of wooden kegs of beer.

Holmes then asked Hamm if he knew of any other brewers who used a different method of refrigeration. Suddenly, the man clammed up. "You'll have to talk to my son about that," he said finally, and rang a bell.

William Hamm was much more congenial than his father. "You'll have to forgive him," the younger Hamm said of his elder. "He tends to live in the past once in a while, especially now that he's in his seventies. And he still holds a grudge, after all these years."

"A grudge against whom?" Holmes asked.

"Jacob Schmidt," said William Hamm. "He was our brewmeister for several years. He helped make this company what it is today. But he left us about twelve years ago, when my father was unable to give him the one thing he wanted most."

"And what was that?" I asked.

"A share of the company," Hamm explained. "Jacob wanted to have his own brewery some day, and becoming part-owner was the best way to get it. But with one son, five sons-in-law and several grandsons, my father couldn't see himself bringing someone from outside the family in to be his partner.

"Our families had been very close," Hamm went on. "Schmidt's only child, Marie, and my baby sister, Emma, were the best of friends, and our parents regularly socialized together. But when Jacob left to become a partner in the North Star Brewery, things soured. He not only took over the company, he turned it into our biggest competitor. Father hasn't spoken to him, or about him, since. He wouldn't even go to Marie's wedding this summer. But I still have a great deal of respect for Jacob, and speak to him often. I'll be happy to answer any questions you have about him."

Holmes asked if Schmidt was using mechanical refrigeration.

"It wouldn't surprise me a bit," was the answer. "His brewery is downstream from ours, so he doesn't have access to the cleanest ice. Plus, he only has one or two caves in that vicinity. He's been yearning to expand, but there's no room at his present location. If you'd like, I can call him, to see if he'll meet with you."

When Holmes said he'd appreciate that, Hamm asked an assistant to give us a quick tour of the brewery while the arrangements were being made. We first saw a huge copper boiler that could hold five hundred bushels of barley at once. The tour guide assured us that Hamm's bought only the best barley and hops it could find, in order to make nothing but the finest quality beer. Once the barley had been cleaned and crushed, it was dropped into the boiler, which reduced it to more than three hundred pounds of juice, called wort. The remaining mash was removed and fed to pigs that Theodore Hamm raised and slaughtered to turn into sausage for employees and friends.

We saw the huge mash vats, the cement floor on which germination took place, the kilns used for drying, and the room where kegs were cleaned and filled. Before the beer made it into kegs, it was aged in huge tanks that held as much as six hundred barrels apiece. During this stage of the process, beech shavings were added to remove impurities, as were hops, for flavor.

We also visited Hamm's brand new bottling plant, where individual brown glass bottles were being filled with beer, crowned, and placed in wooden crates. The popularity of bottled beer was on the rise, not only for at-home consumption but also for resale at ballgames and other public events. Increasingly, brewers were finding an added source of revenue in a service previously provided by grocers and saloon owners. Finally, we were shown an enormous ice-making machine, capable of producing seventy-five tons of ice a day. It was at this point that William Hamm rejoined us.

"I told you, my father still lives in the past," he said of the ice-making process. "It's been a while since Lake Phalen produced enough ice to last us year round. We've had this machine for quite a few years now. It operates on a compression-based system designed by Thaddeus Lowe, the famous balloonist. That puts us a step or two behind Jacob Schmidt, who just informed me that he has recently installed a new mechanical refrigeration system, and it does use a fuel similar to the one being developed by Diesel. He'll be happy to show it to you any time this morning. Now, would you care to visit our tasting room on the way out?"

I was tempted, but Holmes said we had too much to do. We thanked William Hamm for his hospitality, and returned to the street, where Emerson Lewis still waited.

Our next stop was the North Star Brewery. It also was on Dayton's Bluff, a mile or two to the southeast, at the corner of Commercial Street and Hudson Avenue.

Like Theodore Hamm, Jacob Schmidt had immigrated to America from Germany, arriving in Rochester, New York, in 1865, at the ripe age of twenty. He went to work immediately for Miller Brewing Company, and later honed his skills at the Best, Blatz and Schlitz breweries in Milwaukee, before coming to Minnesota. After a stint as foreman of the well-known August Schell Brewery in New Ulm, Jacob Schmidt came to St. Paul to work for Theodore Hamm.

When a St. Paul grocer named William Constans offered not only a share in the North Star Brewery, but also a chance to run it, Schmidt reluctantly left his friend and mentor and took over the Frenchman's beer business. He'd seen it as the opportunity of a lifetime.

"Next to Bavaria, Minnesota is the best place in the world to own a brewery," Schmidt told us upon our meeting him. "You raise some of the world's best grain here, and you have some of the world's purest water, in great abundance. Those are beer's two main ingredients, you know! The city of St. Paul has two more advantages. All of these natural caves along the river are ideal for cooling and aging beer. And the thousands of German immigrants here provide a ready-made market for the product. It's no wonder there are more than a hundred breweries in the state, including a dozen in St. Paul alone."

Without prompting, Schmidt noted that he and James J. Hill shared similar political opinions, especially those against government regulation of small business, and the growth of unions. Again, the name of Archbishop Ireland came up. In addition to the Archbishop's support of the unions' right to strike, Schmidt lambasted Ireland for organizing a temperance union.

"There are eight hundred saloons in this city, most of them family owned and operated," Schmidt exclaimed. "Can you imagine what would happen to the local economy if every one of them was suddenly forced out of business?"

Again, Holmes tried to steer the subject away from politics and back to the topic we'd come to discuss: mechanical refrigeration. Holmes stressed the importance of the discussion by explaining that he hoped Schmidt would be able to lead us to the source of the fuel the killer had used to start the fire—and eventually to the murderer himself. Schmidt asked a foreman to retrieve a sample of the fuel, noting that, to his knowledge, his was the only firm in the city currently using such a substance.

"This new refrigeration system cost more than I'd like," Schmidt complained, as we waited for the fuel sample to arrive, "but we had to try something. We've run out of room to store product. Right now, we have access to only one cave, and at least a third of it is susceptible to seasonal flooding by underground springs, making it unsafe and impractical to use. We'd like to add a bottling plant as well, but the federal government won't let us expand, because of the sacred Indian burial grounds to the south of us."

At that point, the foreman arrived with a sample of the fuel. After Holmes examined it, he asked if any of the men who had access to it were over six feet tall, heavyset and left-handed.

"For that information, you'll have to talk to my plant manager," Schmidt said. "He does most of the hiring here, and also handles the payroll. He knows all of our men, by name and by face."

A few minutes later, we were talking with Adolph Bremer. He, it turns out, was the former bookkeeper who had married Schmidt's daughter, Marie, that summer. Bremer had the answer to Holmes' query.

"Yes, we have two men who meet that description," he said. "Their names are Hermann Oberhauf and Stigvard Mattson."

"Stigvard Mattson, that sounds like a Swedish name," Holmes said. "I got the impression from Herr Hamm that you brewers only hired fellow Germans."

"Well, that depends," Bremer said with a chuckle. "The more recent arrivals from Sweden are a bunch of pansies, trying to escape whatever social ills they imagine they've suffered at the hands of aristocrats. The first Swedes who came here were a hardy lot: fishermen, dairy farmers, dock workers, miners and loggers. Like the Germans, they saw America as the land of opportunity, and in Minnesota, they saw a land that was a lot like their homeland.

"Mattson is one of the hardy ones. I recruited him myself. He was a dock loader down at the levee. When I saw how hard he worked, day after day, I offered him a job. He's been here for years. I can't imagine him, or Big Herm Oberhauf, being involved in a murder. But they're the only men we have who fit your description. Shall I call them in?"

"No, I'm not ready to question them yet," Holmes replied. "I need to learn more about them first. I'd like to look at your records, if I may, then check the police blotters as well. I might even want to tail them for an evening or two. Peter, are you up to helping me with that?"

"You bet!" I said. At last, I was going to get to do some actual detective work!

"Well, I have to meet with a supplier in a few minutes," Bremer said, "but if you come to my office around half past four, I'll point them out to you, and give you all the information I have on them. In the meantime, if you want to blend in, I'd suggest you both go to a pawn shop and buy an old double-breasted box coat. It's what all the workers seem to be wearing this winter."

CHAPTER 14

LITTLE GERMANY

On the way back from Schmidt's brewery, we stopped at a pawn shop to buy two box coats, as Adolph Bremer had suggested. Then we returned to the Grand for lunch. Afterward, it was my turn to nap, while Holmes moved his gear back to the Ryan Hotel. By four o'clock, I'd taken a streetcar to the Ryan, and together we took a cab to the North Star Brewery.

As promised, Bremer told us what he could about our two suspects.

"Tiny Oberhauf has worked here nearly ten years," he said, looking at his files. "He works in the room where the kegs are cleaned and refilled, then helps move them to the aging stage. We recently were able to buy a small warehouse next door, which is where we installed the new cooling system, so of course he has access to the fuel. He's a family man, very jovial, and well-liked by all the other workers. He lives in the Bohemian neighborhood, beyond the upper levee, just off Fort Road. I have his address for you.

"As I believe I've already mentioned, I hired Stig Mattson myself, three or four years ago. He's been a hard worker, as I anticipated. He helps load the delivery wagons, hauling beer from both the warehouse next door, where the refrigeration system is, and the two caverns beneath us. Far as I know, he has no family. He's a bit of a loner, and is one of the few who don't mind going down into the cave. He lists his home as Railroad Island."

"Railroad Island, where is that?" Holmes asked.

"It's a triangular area, north of East Seventh Street and west of Payne Avenue," Bremer explained. "It's surrounded by railroads on all three sides, which is how it got its name.

"It's where most of the Swedes live," Bremer went on, "even those who work downriver in the slaughter houses and meat-packing plants. If you're planning to go there, I hope you speak Swedish. That's all you'll hear along Snoose Boulevard. You'd better have a liking for strong coffee, too, along with pickled herring and lutefisk."

"Lutefisk, yuk!" I exclaimed.

"Sounds like I'd better take Mattson," Holmes said. "My Swedish is a bit rusty, but at least Herr Oberhauf should be going home in Peter's direction."

"I'll point them out as they leave, and you can fall in with the crowd," Bremer said. "Most of the men will be walking up Plum Street to Maria Avenue, one block away. There's a trio of horse-drawn streetcars there that will take them up to the main line on Seventh Street. Here, you'll need these."

"What is it?" I asked, as I examined the small coin-shaped piece of wood he'd given me.

"It's a chit for the streetcar," Bremer replied. "We give each man one at the end of his shift. It's good for one hour. If he goes straight home to his wife and family, he gets a free ride. If he uses the token to go to a tavern, he's on his own. There's Tiny Oberhauf now, the big fellow with the full beard. You can tell from his nickname what a great sense of humor he has."

Whoa! He won't be hard to follow in a crowd, I thought to myself. Had Tiny's bushy black beard been white, he could have passed for Santa Claus. Oberhauf, who looked to be about forty years old, was well over six feet tall, and had to tip the scales at two-fifty or better. He reminded me of Big Ahl Neunen, but even bigger, and softer, around the belly. His waddling gait told me I'd have no trouble keeping up with him.

Just before I left, I got a glimpse of Stigvard Mattson. The Swede appeared to be in his early fifties, with short-cropped white hair, and a neatly trimmed handlebar moustache. He was just over six feet tall, and solidly built. I quickly realized that neither of our two suspects would have had any trouble breaking down Brower's storeroom door. I noticed, too, that both were wearing cheap boots, similar to those Holmes had been investigating.

My first night as a detective turned out to be nothing like I thought it would be. In our old box coats, Holmes and I fit right into the crowd milling toward Maria Avenue. When we got there, Mattson climbed onto the first wagon, with Holmes right behind. Tiny hung around for a while, joking with his mates, until we both caught the last trolley to leave.

At Seventh Street, we switched cars and rode all the way through the lowertown area, past Seven Corners and out the Fort Road, to that part of town known as Little Germany. When my man finally got off, I rode to the next corner. I knew I'd have no trouble doubling back to catch up with him.

Sure enough, I saw his huge body trudging down a side street. I followed a block and a half behind, until he turned and headed up the front steps of a small bungalow. I walked slowly past, and took up my post behind a huge oak tree across the corner. I could see him through the kitchen window as he kissed his wife, then sat down to eat dinner with her and three children. It reminded me that I hadn't eaten yet!

After dinner he went into the next room to lie down on the couch. Despite the youngest child climbing on him every few minutes, the man seemed to sleep like a baby. Now I was not only hungry, but sleepy as well. And cold! After an hour, my teeth were chattering. I was almost ready to give up, when the man got up and went upstairs. Maybe now I can go someplace warm, and get something to eat, I thought. As soon as his bedroom light goes out.

But when the light went out in the upstairs dormer, the man came back downstairs, dressed in the most garish waistcoat I'd ever seen. He hugged his kids, kissed his wife again, pulled on his overcoat, and headed out into the cold, dark night.

Having already used his free chit, Oberhauf ignored the streetcars that passed him by, and marched back up Seventh Street for more than a mile. Finally, he reached the CSPS Hall on Michigan Avenue, and went inside. I waited about ten minutes, until my fingers were numb, then went inside myself.

"Gemutlichkeit" is a word I've heard the Germans use, and I can't think of a better word to describe what I saw that night. There was a huge room, filled with people, and they all seemed to know each other, like one big, happy family. The fellowship was beyond social, maybe even beyond festive. Everyone was laughing, singing or dancing, sometimes all three at once. There was beer everywhere, coming in a steady flow from a bar at one end of the room. At the other end was a stage, occupied by a rowdy polka band. It featured a piano accordion, a button squeeze-box, a bass horn and drums.

"Five Fat Deutschmen" it said on the huge bass drum. Despite the band's name, there were just four musicians on the stage. Only one of them was fat—big, jolly, Tiny Oberhauf. He appeared to be having a ball, as did everyone around him.

One tune after another, the band played on: mostly polkas, a schottische or two, an occasional waltz. The assembled throng danced and danced. Once or twice, Tiny stepped to the front of the stage to sing, and the crowd went wild.

I had a mug of hot cider to warm up, then eventually switched to lager. After a while, I'd gotten to know the bartender, Otto, well enough to chat him up.

"Is everybody here German?" I asked him.

"Nein," he laughed, looking over the crowd. "Mostly Czechs and Slovaks, a few Poles—but they all love the German music!"

"Yeah, I love the band, too," I said. "Do they play here often?"

"Every Monday, Wednesday and Friday night," he said, between slinging drinks.

"How late do they go?" I asked the next time he came by.

"They quit at midnight during the week, 'cuz most of 'em gotta go to work the next day," Otto said. "On weekends, they don't wind down 'til one or two o'clock."

"What about last Friday, the night of the fire, were they here that night?" I asked. I tried to act nonchalant, dipping my giant salted pretzel in a porringer of hot, melted cheese.

"Oh, yeah, that was a late one," Otto replied. "The band was playing so loud, I barely heard the hook-and-ladder clang by at two in the morning." I had the feeling the bartender was starting to get suspicious of me, but I had to ask one more question.

"What about the big guy, was he still here then?" I asked about Oberhauf. I was right, I had gone one step too far. I was new at this detective stuff. It wasn't as easy as it looked!

"Young fella, you're sure asking a lot of questions," Otto said. "Why do you wanna know?"

I had to think for a minute. Finally, I shook my head, and said, "I don't know, I just thought I'd seen him somewhere else that night."

"Well, you're wrong, sonny," Otto said. "Tiny was here all night."

"You're sure?" I asked, pressing my luck.

"Of course I'm sure," Otto said indignantly. "You can't have an oompahpah band without a tuba player! Now, do you want another beer, or not?"

He didn't get an answer. I was already out the door, heading back to my warm, cozy bed at the Grand. I knew I'd sleep well that night. Over the past few hours, I'd grown fond of Hermann Tiny Oberhauf. I was relieved, and delighted, to find out that he could not have been our killer.

CHAPTER 15

SWEDE HOLLOW

The next morning, Holmes and I met at the Boardman, where Brower had taken a suite down the hall from Chaney's. Following back-to-back meetings with his insurance agent and the chief of detectives on Monday morning, the Superintendent had made a quick round-trip to St. Cloud. He'd returned with enough clothes to get him through the week. He hoped this body-in-the-basement business would be wrapped up in time for the wedding. So did I!

Brower listened intently as I told about my previous evening. Then Holmes took his turn.

Mattson and Holmes had ridden the horse car up Maria to Seventh, then switched to the main line and headed down into lowertown. "It was the busiest time of day, with people getting on and off at every corner," Holmes explained. "I had no trouble blending in with the crowd."

At Wabasha, Mattson disembarked and walked two blocks south, to Foley's Billiards Parlor. "Again," Holmes said, "there were workers and shoppers everywhere. Just to be safe, I walked on by, to the next corner, and doubled back before going in."

That, he said, was almost a mistake. Once inside, there was no sign of Stig Mattson. Holmes gave us a quick description of the scene, with his usual eye for detail. There were six billiard tables, all occupied by players of various skills. Sometimes two to a table, sometimes four, they all bantered with one another in a mostly jovial manner, often setting their cue sticks aside to drink or smoke between shots. The air was filled with smoke, and with laughter.

There was a bar that ran the full length of the room. The bar, like the tables, was full, from one end to the other. Most of the men appeared to have just gotten off work. Others had been there for a while, judging from their stages of dress, which ranged from topcoats and hats to waistcoats and shirt sleeves. Other than an occasional catcall to a new arrival, the men at the bar were absorbed in their drinks, or in conversation with their mates, or both. They paid little attention to those at the tables.

Holmes, on the other hand, was taking the measure of every man in the place. He eyed them all, from one end of the room to the other, but still no sign of Mattson. Holmes said he was about to give up and ask one of the bartenders, when he saw two well-dressed men come in the side door and head up a back stairway. He bought a beer, hung his hat and coat on the antlers of a moose head mounted on a wall near the stairs, and headed up.

At the top of the stairs, he found himself again in a billiard parlor, but one entirely different from the one just below. Here, there were only two tables. There were two players at each, and they were dead serious. All around them, men stood against the wall, or around tall, tiny tables, and watched intently. Here, as below, the room was filled with smoke. But for great periods of time, the only sounds to be heard were the clacking of one ivory ball hitting another, and the rare grunt of appreciation, or disgust.

Periodically, a man in a green waistcoat would announce a score. There would be a polite round of applause, perhaps accompanied by groans or a cussword, and money would change hands among the observers. The men who were the center of attention, it turns out, were professional pool players. The men around the perimeter of the room were bettors, wagering on the outcome of each match. Who would've thunk it, in lowertown St. Paul?

It didn't take Holmes long to spot Mattson. He was among the gamblers. And, for the time being, at least, he was among the winners. Holmes watched him pocket a handful of bills.

Not wishing to look out of place, Holmes picked out a table where the wagering seemed low-stakes and relatively friendly, and joined in the action. It allowed him to keep an eye on the

Swede, who had put his money on a man named Cochrane. The latter had little trouble beating all comers, including a man named Townsend, who appeared to be a local favorite.

During the next two hours, Holmes said he watched Mattson rake in more than two hundred dollars. A good two months' pay for someone in his position! But, like most gamblers, he didn't know when to quit. Instead of taking his winnings back to Railroad Island, Mattson took them to the bar downstairs, where he bought several rounds of drinks. Then he made an even bigger mistake. Instead of wagering his money on Cochrane, a man of considerable skill and talent, he began betting on his own skill and talent, which were nothing to brag about.

Within an hour, a pool cue in one hand and a steady flow of drinks in the other, Stig Mattson lost every penny he'd won that night, and then some. By the time he left Foley's, he didn't have a nickel for the streetcar, and set out for home on foot.

With most of the after-work crowd now home in bed, following Mattson undetected became more of a challenge. "You have to remain a good distance behind, sometimes on one side of the street, sometimes the other," Holmes had told me that afternoon. "Every block or two, do what you can to change your appearance: remove your hat for a while; change its shape before you put it back on; take your coat off and carry it, unseen if possible; alter your gait, the way you swing your arms; slouch, adapt a limp, anything to change your silhouette if he looks back. Walk fast enough to nearly catch up, then disappear around a corner. When you reappear, make sure your look has changed, and walk more slowly."

Remaining a good distance behind Mattson was not a problem, Holmes said, because every ten minutes or so, the big Swede would jump onto the rear platform of a passing streetcar and ride a block or two for free, until the conductor kicked him off. Holmes had to race to keep up. The last time it happened, he said, was near the foot of Dayton's Bluff.

"Trying to remain in the shadows," Holmes explained, "I raced up East Seventh Street to Payne Avenue and looked north, toward Railroad Island, assuming that's where he had headed. He was nowhere in sight. For the second time that night, I feared I'd lost him."

On a hunch, Holmes passed by Payne and continued up East Seventh. Halfway across the Seventh Street Improvement Arches, he looked down from the bridge and saw a lone figure, walking north along the railroad tracks. It was Mattson.

"I raced back to the foot of the bridge, and slid down the hill, ripping my box coat in the process," Holmes explained. "When I reached the bottom of the hill, my prey was no longer in sight. Thanks to the moonlight, I was able to follow his tracks in the snow. They led me to a sight I wouldn't have believed if I hadn't seen it with my own eyes."

He then described heading up a snow-covered dirt trail into a world very different from the one he'd just left. From the banks of the winding little creek that bisected the deep valley, hundreds of homemade shacks sprung up, littering both sides of the steep ravine. There were no streets, no sidewalks, only a single, meandering trail. There were no yards to speak of, beyond fenced-in pens for chickens or pigs. The shanties had been built with scrap materials. A closer look told him there was no electricity, no running water. The only toilets were tiny outhouses, built on stilts right over the creek, which provided primitive plumbing for the inhabitants.

"That's Swede Hollow," Brower told him. "The Swedes call it Svenske Dahlen."

"Where I come from, we'd call it a slum," Holmes said.

"Our civic leaders prefer to call it a stepping-stone community," Brower explained, with some disdain. "To the dismay of Archbishop Ireland, the Irish have a similar settlement, called the Connemara Patch, just south of the Arches, between Seventh and Fourth Streets.

"Swede Hollow, be as it may, is where most of the Swedish immigrants go when they first get off the train at Union Depot," Brower continued. "They follow the railroad tracks up the hollow until they find an empty shack, or one occupied by someone they know, and move right in. Most of them only stay there until they find a decent job and can afford to move up the hill to Railroad Island. It takes some longer than others."

"And some," Holmes said, "apparently end up moving back there—especially if they've fallen victim to alcohol and gambling." It was obvious he was talking about Mattson.

"So what did you learn about him?" I asked. "Could he be our man?"

"I know that he was not at Foley's on Friday night," Holmes said. "The croupier was quite certain of that. His man, Cochrane, cleaned house that night. Mattson wasn't there to take advantage of it, which was quite unusual, enough so to be noticed. I'll know more in an hour or two, after I return to search his shack while he's at work."

"And how do you intend to do that, in broad daylight?" I asked.

"I still have the disguise I wore on Saturday night," Holmes said. "There are plenty of vagrants moving about the Hollow. I don't think one more will attract much attention."

"After that, I'd appreciate it if you'd speak with Chief O'Connor again," Brower said. "Unless you come up with a more likely suspect, I'm afraid I'm still at the top of his list."

"Really?" Holmes asked, sounding surprised.

"After I spoke with him yesterday," Brower explained, "he told me not to leave town. When I said it was absolutely necessary that I make a quick trip to St. Cloud, he sent a man along with me, to ensure my return. He wants to see me again at eleven this morning. I'd be forever in your debt if you could accompany me."

"It would be my pleasure," Holmes said. "Don't worry about a thing. I'll meet with your chief of detectives, and we'll straighten this matter out once and for all."

That turned out to be easier said than done.

CHAPTER 16

BULL REDUX

Later that morning, Holmes and I accompanied Brower to police headquarters. The chief of detectives was expecting us.

"Have you come to confess?" the Bull asked Brower as soon as we arrived.

"Now see here," Holmes cut in. "I've told you before, sir, I object to this line of questioning. Surely you don't continue to suspect Mr. Brower of murder?"

"At the moment, I have no other suspects—unless you've brought me one," O'Connor said.

"We'll get to that momentarily," Holmes said. "First, please have the courtesy to answer my question. Do you really suspect Mr. Brower of murder?"

"Let me show you something," the Bull said, peeling the cover off an easel that stood next to his desk. On the easel was a painting. The subject was a Union officer, astride a rearing gray stallion, surrounded by savages in warpaint.

"Do you recognize him?" O'Connor asked Brower.

"It's General Sibley, at the Battle of Wood Lake," the Superintendent said.

"Look at his hands," the chief of detectives said. In his right hand, the soldier held a smoking sidearm. In his left, he was wielding a saber.

"You served in Company D of the First Regiment of Sibley's Mounted Rangers, did you not?" O'Connor asked Brower. The Superintendent nodded affirmatively.

"Did they train you all to fight like this?" O'Connor asked.

"In close-quartered, hand-to-hand combat, yes," Brower confirmed.

"So," O'Connor said, counting off each point: "On the night of the murder, sir, you have no alibi. You fit the physical description, provided by Mr. Holmes himself, of the murderer. It now appears that you also had the means. Is there any reason why I should not arrest you?"

"Because there is no motive," Holmes interjected. "You have not established a link between the Superintendent and the victim—because no such link exists."

"I'm working on that," O'Connor replied. "Mr. Brower, how well did you know Mrs. Jane Grey Swisshelm?"

"By reputation only," Brower replied. The question had caught him by surprise.

"Were you not in the newspaper business yourself?" O'Connor asked.

"Briefly, yes, but not until after the War," Brower said. "Mrs. Swisshelm had moved back east by then. Her nephew had taken over her newspaper in St. Cloud."

"In what year did you move to the city of St. Cloud?"

"In 1873," Brower answered.

"May I ask where this is headed?" Holmes asked.

"Before moving to Fargo, our victim, Padraig Doherty, lived in St. Cloud," O'Connor said. "He got his start in the printing business as a stick-boy for Mrs. Swisshelm's newspaper."

"What's a stick-boy?" I asked.

"The person who arranges wooden or lead type in a compositor stick," Brower explained, "before it's placed in a printer's case and rolled flat, for the platen." Turning to O'Connor, Brower added, "I understood that Will Mitchell started out as his aunt's stick-boy."

"Yes, but not her first one," O'Connor said. "That would have been Padraig Doherty."

"Whom you still have not linked to Mr. Brower," Holmes pointed out.

"No, you're right," O'Connor admitted. "The timelines don't seem to match up."

"Then I'll ask you for a third time," Holmes said. "Is Mr. Brower still a suspect?"

"I'm still convinced that the crime is somehow linked to him, whether he knows it or not," O'Connor said, not really answering the question.

"How could that be?" Holmes asked.

"As the Superintendent implied in our earlier interview," the Bull replied, "he has stepped on a number of toes over the years, acquiring an impressive list of would-be enemies. Thomas Jefferson we can forget, he's been dead for seventy years. James Gordon Bennett is still alive and kicking. What's your quarrel with him?" O'Connor asked Brower.

"My gosh, that goes back twenty years," Brower recalled. "Sometime in the 1870s, a young reporter named Julius Chambers, from Bennett's New York Herald, alleged in his newspaper column to have journeyed from the source of the Mississippi to its mouth. When I repudiated his claim, he disparaged Joseph Nicollet, and we got into a heck of a brouhaha. But we eventually made up. Last I heard, he was writing about romance on the Sargasso Sea."

"And last I heard," Holmes said to O'Connor, "Bennett was in Europe, trying to figure out how to circumvent the transatlantic cable. A dispute over the source of the Mississippi would appear to be the least of his worries. Who's next on your list?"

"Willard Glazier," O'Connor said. "I understand the historical society also had problems with him?"

"Actually, it was Glazier's brother who got upset," Brower said. "In the early 1880s, Glazier claimed to have visited a source beyond any cited by either Nicollet or Schoolcraft. But it was General James Baker who quashed that claim. The Glaziers have no beef with me."

"Alright, then," the Bull said, "what about this business involving the estate of Alfred Hill?"

Hill, I knew, had been a member of the Minnesota Historical Society. He was also patron of the Northwestern Archaeological Survey. For years, a man named Theodore Hayes Lewis had done field work for Hill, often collaborating with Brower. When Hill died unexpectedly in June of 1895, without a will, the future of the archaeological survey, and its holdings, became subject of a lawsuit.

Despite a surprise court appearance by a mysterious young lady who claimed to have been engaged to the elderly Hill, the court ruled that the entirety of Hill's estate, including all the survey findings, belonged to Hill's nearest relatives—two elderly cousins, one in England and one in Canada.

In correspondence with Brower, Lewis said he could not bear the thought of his life's work ending up "buried in oblivion in someone's garret," or worse yet, sold to some museum in a foreign land, where its "valuable contribution to the knowledge of prehistoric America" would go unappreciated. He enlisted Brower to try to encourage Hill's cousins to donate the survey findings to the historical society. So far, those efforts had failed.

"I can't imagine either of those two old widows sending a hit man after me," Brower told the Bull. "As for the fraudulent fiancée, now you might be on to something. I'm sure there was more to that story than what we heard in court. She may have had some nefarious contacts, who could still be trying to profit from Hill's death."

"I already have someone trying to track down the young lady," the Bull said. "For your sake, Mr. Brower, I hope we get to the bottom of this soon. Now, Mr. Holmes, please be so kind as to bring me up to date on what you have been doing."

Holmes gave the chief of detectives a brief summary of our visits to the Hill Mansion and the two breweries, and of our efforts to tail our two suspects. He noted that Hermann Oberhauf had an air-tight alibi for the night of the murder, but that Stigvard Mattson did not.

"Mattson, eh?" the Bull said. "The name sounds familiar. Let me check our files."

In a moment, O'Connor returned with a very thin folder. "We have only two entries on him. One appears to have been self defense: he cold-cocked a meat-packer who'd pulled a dirk on him in a saloon. Six months later, he had to be forcibly evicted from his home in Railroad Island, for falling behind on his rent. He seems to have quite a temper, and has had a run of bad luck lately, but so far has managed to keep himself out of jail. Shall I call him in?"

"Not just yet," Holmes said. "I've searched his shanty in Swede Hollow, and found nothing to tie him to the murder, other than the fuel he steals from work to heat the place. There was no sign of anything resembling a murder weapon. And like Mr. Brower, he has no apparent ties to the victim—at least, none that I've found so far. With no family, no home to speak of, and a less than enviable job, he has nothing to hold him here. If he's spooked, he may run. I'd like to take a shot at getting inside his head, if you could give me another day or two?"

"Based on your reputation, Mr. Holmes, I'm willing to give you the benefit of the doubt," O'Connor said. "Just keep this in mind: Until we come up with something better, your friend, Brower, remains under suspicion, regardless of my personal respect for him."

"I understand," Holmes said. "Now, before we part, would you mind telling me what kind of hold you have on Herr Mueller?"

"He's a hustler," O'Connor replied. "He takes unsuspecting pigeons from out-of-town and fleeces them. We can't have that in our city. When a salesman from Chicago or St. Louis or Milwaukee brings his hard-earned money to town, we want to make sure he feels comfortable here. We don't want to scare him off to Minneapolis. We'd like to make him want to come back to St. Paul."

"That explains the prevalence of brothels and gambling dens, I assume," Holmes said.

"Everything in its place, my good man, everything in its place," O'Connor replied. I thought he'd be insulted, but he wasn't.

With that, we left police headquarters and headed to lunch. Holmes had not succeeded in getting Brower off the hook. But he had bought him more time.

CHAPTER 17

THE GAME

B rower, at least somewhat relieved, went to have lunch with his insurance agent. Holmes and I decided to try the Market Place. Over sandwiches, I asked Holmes how he planned to get inside Stig Mattson's head.

"I intend to gain his confidence," Holmes said.

"And how will you do that?"

"By taking advantage of his weaknesses," Holmes explained. "His inclination toward mixing alcohol and gambling, coupled with his limited skill at billiards, make him an easy target. He'll get in over his head again tonight, and when he does, I'll come to his rescue. That will put me in good stead with him, perhaps enough to get him to confide in me."

"How will you come to his rescue, as you say?" I asked.

"With a billiards cue, of course," Holmes replied.

"Do you play?"

"I have observed Watson and his friend, Thurston, play the game on numerous occasions, more than enough to pick up the mannerisms," Holmes replied. "As for what happens on the surface of the table, it appears to be little more than simple Euclidian geometry, based on the congruence of angles. Throw in a little military strategy—defensive positioning, that sort of thing—and you have it."

"There's also the matter of controlling the cue ball," I protested. "You have to know how much and what kind of spin to put on it—that sort of thing."

"And what is that called, if I may ask?" Holmes had a gleam in his eye.

I suddenly realized why. I hung my head as I sheepishly replied: "English."

"Ah, I see," he said with a grin. "In that case, I think I should be able to handle it. Besides, I have another trick or two up my sleeve. You'll have to wait until tonight to see what they are. Right now, I have an appointment with a young lady."

An appointment with a lady? Now that was an unexpected development! I tried to get him to tell me more, but he just laughed me off. All afternoon, I tried to imagine what Holmes was up to, and with whom. Could it be someone from one of those brothels he mentioned? Well before the appointed hour, I went to his room at the Ryan. The lady in question was just leaving. It turned out to be the maid who'd served us coffee and tea at the Hill Mansion. Now what the devil was she doing there?

Holmes couldn't help but notice the curious look on my face. "Helge has been helping me brush up on my Swedish," he explained, with a twinkle in his eye. "What did you think she was doing here?" I could feel the blood rush to my cheeks.

We headed downstairs to the Ryan's dining room. Unlike most of our meals together, which had consisted of light sandwiches or soups, on this night we went whole hog. "We may have to quaff a few beers as part of our subterfuge tonight," Holmes said. "Best to do so on a full stomach, so you don't get lightheaded."

I was stuffed by the time we were ready to head for Foley's. As we rose to leave the dining room, we were approached by none other than Bull O'Connor.

"We've finally found Fifi," he told us.

Holmes waited, then asked, "And Fifi is . . . ?

"The fraudulent fiancée of Alfred Hill, of course," the Chief said. "She registered with the court as Francine DuBois. Fifi is her . . . stage name."

"She's a performer, then?" Holmes inquired.

"Of sorts," O'Connor replied, with a sly grin. "She works for Nina Clifford."

"And Miss Clifford is . . . ?" It was clear that Holmes was growing impatient with this conversation.

"The proprietor of a . . . gentlemen's club, around the corner from the police station," came the reply. It was equally clear that O'Connor enjoyed being the purveyor of tiny parcels of information.

"I see," said Holmes. "And what is the significance of this find?"

"Miss DuBois," the Chief explained deliberately, "in return for the police dropping certain charges against her, has agreed to supply information which may have some bearing on our case."

"Would you care to share that information?" Holmes asked. Getting information from the Bull was like pulling porcupine prickles out of your hinder—slow and painful.

"It seems," said O'Connor, "that one of her regular visitors has been bragging about a caper he pulled the evening of the fire."

"A caper?" said Holmes. "What sort of a caper?"

"We haven't been able to track down the gentleman yet, so we don't know all the details," O'Connor said. "But the man in question fits your description of the culprit: he's over six feet tall, and built like an ox."

"What else do you know about him?" asked Holmes, his interest obviously piqued.

"His name is Johnny Tomasko, a former boxer," the Chief continued. "Klaus Mueller remembers him as the Two-Fisted Tomato, because he could lead or follow with his left hand or his right—though not very effectively with either."

"Ambidextrous, eh?" said Holmes. "That's three strikes against him, then." Recalling the Rule of Threes that Holmes had told me about ten years earlier, I realized that Johnny Tomasko had suddenly become a prime suspect, right up there with Stig Mattson—and the Superintendent.

"There's more," said O'Connor.

"And what might that be?" Holmes asked, trying to hide his exasperation.

The Bull was finally ready to deliver his punch line. "Police records show," he said slowly, "that Tomasko is the lug who pulled a dirk on Mattson—who promptly rewarded him with a haymaker left hook."

"So," Holmes summarized, mimicking the Bull's tedious delivery, "you're thinking that Tomasko could be the real killer; that he's trying to frame Mattson for the crime, in order to get even for an earlier altercation. Is that correct?"

"Exactly," O'Connor said, smugly.

"Well, good luck finding him," Holmes said, as if he felt O'Connor wasn't up to the task.

"Oh, that shouldn't be too difficult," the Bull said. "Miss DuBois assures us that Johnny and his pals are nightly regulars at the Bucket of Blood saloon, at the foot of Washington Street. We're headed down that way right now, to haul him in for questioning."

And we, despite this new twist, were headed to Foley's Billiards Parlor, according to plan. Once there, we bellied up to the downstairs bar.

"Shouldn't we be going upstairs, where the action is?" I asked.

"I already know what's happening up there," Holmes said. "What's important is what will happen down here later. In the meantime, it's best not to draw attention to ourselves."

With Christmas Eve just two nights away, the place wasn't as busy as I expected. We chatted at the bar for a while. When a billiards table opened up, Holmes suggested that we grab it. I had played quite a bit in college, but Holmes more than held his own against me. If he was, indeed, a newcomer to the game, it didn't show. We'd won three games apiece, and were in the midst of a rubber match, when the regulars from upstairs began to filter down to the bar.

Sure enough, Stig Mattson had once again backed a winner. He immediately bought a round of drinks for the house. After a couple of rounds, he gravitated toward the billiards tables. It didn't take long for him to find a challenger. To my surprise, it was none other than Klaus Mueller! Holmes told me later that he'd gotten Chief O'Connor to give the Mauler a special one-night reprieve from his hustling ban. It soon became obvious why the German had been barred from playing at the local billiards parlors.

It was fun to watch Mueller at work. He was obviously quite skilled. Yet he never gave the impression that he was unbeatable. He regularly displayed just enough chinks in his armor to lead his opponent to believe that the Mauler could be had. When he made an exceptionally good shot, he sheepishly acted as if it were nothing but luck. Stig Mattson, in high spirits to start with after his winning night at the gambling table, his confidence further buoyed by frequent rounds of drink, fell right into the trap.

After little more than an hour, Mattson had frittered away all his winnings, and was digging himself into a hole. A couple of times during breaks in the action, Holmes had commiserated with the man in Swedish. He was merely dangling the bait. Now it was time to set the hook.

"How much do you owe?" Holmes asked the Swede.

"A hundred dollars," was the reply.

"How about I help you get it back?" Holmes asked.

"And why would you do that?" Mattson asked. He was rightfully suspicious, but alcohol had clouded his judgment.

"I hate those Hun bastards," Holmes said coldly. Mattson handed over his cue.

"I'll play you for this man's debt," Holmes then said to Mueller, "double or nothing, what do you say?"

"I'd say you were a fool," the Mauler replied.

"That remains to be seen," Holmes said. "Do you accept the challenge?"

"With pleasure," Mueller said, chalking his cue. "We'll play to two hundred points—a dollar a button on the side."

"Agreed," said Holmes. The game was afoot.

Mueller won the draw. On the opening spread, the ivories rolled into perfect position for him, and he methodically ran the table. The second spread was much the same. Only after a string of twenty-five points did he miss a short draw for position, giving Holmes his first chance to play. He responded with an impressive opening string of seventeen, before turning the table back to the German.

For the next hour or so, the game followed a similar pattern, with Herr Mueller slowly but surely pulling away. After four exchanges, he had all but doubled up on Holmes. By now, Mattson was off sulking in a corner, second-guessing his decision to trust a stranger—even one who spoke flawless Swedish.

But then, almost imperceptibly, things started to change. The ivories began rolling better for Holmes. His best runs steadily climbed from seventeen to twenty to twenty-two. Mueller, on the other hand, began to find himself more frequently in poor position. In response to the steady improvement of Holmes, the German could manage a string no higher than fifteen.

Once Holmes pulled back into a tie, the game began in earnest. Everyone remaining in the bar at that hour, including Mattson, turned their attention to the match. From that point on, the lead alternated from man to man. No more than a handful of buttons separated them at any exchange, until the final string—when Holmes pulled away by ten.

It had been impossible for me to tell whether Holmes had won fair and square, or if Mueller had purposely taken a fall. It's possible the German had just been out of practice, thanks to the hiatus he'd been forced to take as a result of his arrangement with O'Connor. Holmes never told me if there had been some sort of pre-game agreement. And I never asked.

Either way, when I left Foley's Billiards Parlor that night, Holmes and Mattson were at the end of the bar, chatting privately in Swedish over a celebratory round of drinks. It appeared that Holmes had succeeded in gaining Mattson's confidence. Whether he'd been able to get inside the man's head remained to be seen.

CHAPTER 18

GRANITE CITY

By ten o'clock the next morning, Holmes and I were on a train to St. Cloud. An hour earlier, we had met with Chief O'Connor at police headquarters, where the two detectives compared notes on their respective suspects.

The Bull went first. "Since we last spoke," he said to Holmes "we've learned quite a bit about Johnny Tomasko, including a few details which you might find interesting."

"Such as?" Holmes asked, after a pregnant pause. Here we go again, I thought!

"Two weeks ago," O'Connor explained, "Tomasko's right hand was mangled in a meat-processing accident. If he did kill Peg-Leg Paddy, he did it with his left hand, as you predicted."

Holmes nodded. "Anything else?" he asked.

"Yes," O'Connor said. He paused before continuing. "The slaughterhouse where Johnny works has been testing a new refrigeration system, similar to the one recently installed by Jacob Schmidt. I've sent a man there this morning to pick up a sample of the fuel, for analysis."

"Congratulations, Chief," Holmes said, though he didn't sound very sincere. "It sounds like you have your man. Have you arrested him yet?"

"No," the Bull had to admit. "Tomasko claims he was nowhere near the Schutte Building on Friday night. We're keeping him in custody while we check out his alibi. In the meantime, I've been looking into your suspect's background as well, and I have some information which may be helpful to you."

"I would appreciate it very much if you would share it with me," Holmes said. This time, he sounded sincere.

"As you know," the Bull began, "when Adolph Bremer hired him to come to work for the North Star Brewery, Stig Mattson was employed as a dock worker down at the levee. He'd been brought to St. Paul by Anson Northup, who hired him to work on his steamboat line here. Northup had found Mattson in Sauk Rapids, where he'd been a hawser."

"What's a hawser?" I had asked.

"A person who works the hawse line, helping to pull a steam boat upriver, through rapids," said Brower, who'd accompanied us to police headquarters.

"Anyhow," continued O'Connor, "here's the interesting part: Before settling in Sauk Rapids, Mattson had grown up in St. Cloud—in the same neighborhood as Padraig Doherty."

"Now, that is interesting!" said Holmes. "I thank you for that, Chief. And I think I know what the fatal link between Mattson and Doherty might be. Superintendent Brower, do you know if Jane Grey Swisshelm had a younger sister, or a daughter, living in St. Cloud?"

"She had a sister there, but they were pretty close to the same age," Brower said. "She may also have had a child, though I don't remember if it was a boy or a girl. Why do you ask?"

"Last night," Holmes explained, "though I saved him from going further into debt, I was not able to get any information of value out of Mr. Mattson. However, I did get a glimpse of a miniature daguerreotype in the casing of his pocket watch."

"And . . . ?" we all wondered.

"Though many years younger," Holmes answered, "the woman in the photo was the spitting image of the woman in the portrait that hung behind Superintendent Brower's desk—the woman he identified to me as Mrs. Swisshelm."

"Are you sure?" Brower asked.

"Absolutely," Holmes said. "She had the same high forehead, the same hair, the prominent nose, the small mouth, the same haunting, liquid eyes. It had to be a close blood relative."

"Again," Brower said, "I wouldn't know. But I know someone who would: Will Mitchell."

"He was Mrs. Swisshelm's nephew, as I recall?" Holmes asked.

"That's right, her sister's boy," Brower said. "He took over Mrs. Swisshelm's newspaper, the St. Cloud Visiter, when she moved back east after the Sioux Uprising. I got to know him quite well over the next few years. He was secretary of the Minnesota Editorial Association when I was with the Todd County Argus, and he was that organization's president when I ran the Sauk Centre Tribune. I'd be happy to contact him if you'd like."

That's how Holmes ended up on the train to St. Cloud. Of course, I couldn't pass up a chance to drop in on Becky and her mother, so I joined him. On the way, I told Holmes what I knew about William Mitchell, based on my college days in St. Cloud.

"Mitchell was in the newspaper business about thirty-five years," I explained. "After that, he got into real estate, and then banking. He's also been involved in a number of civic projects. They included financing the construction of a dam across the Mississippi that supplies electrical power to the entire city of St. Cloud, and most of the surrounding area."

"Once again, Peter, I am amazed at your knowledge," Holmes offered.

"Well, Mr. Mitchell was also the resident director at St. Cloud Normal while I was there," I had to confess. "He and his wife have several daughters, including at least a couple around my age. They have a huge home, right on the north edge of campus. Their third-floor gym sort of became the center of our social life for a few years. I'm happy to make a return visit."

Before I knew it, we were there. The three-story red brick house at 508 First Avenue South was just as I remembered it: noisy, and full of college kids. Billy Lee, the former slave who'd been the Mitchell family's gardener for thirty years, was shoveling snow from the front walk.

"Master Peter, is that you?" he said, squinting at me as we approached. "Master William just came home for lunch. I'm sure he'll be delighted to see you!"

Over lunch, Will Mitchell told Holmes how he'd gotten started in the newspaper business.

"In May of 1858, just a week after Minnesota became a state, I turned fifteen years old, and my father told me it was time to go out and find a job," Mitchell recalled. "All that summer, I worked as a chainman on the surveying crew that was laying out Minnesota's first-ever state road. Talk about a boring job! One hundred links to a chain, eighty chain lengths to a mile. If your math is still a bit fuzzy, Peter, that works out to sixty-six feet per chain length, times eighty, for every mile between here and Breckenridge, on the Red River of the North.

"After a summer like that," Mitchell went on, "I jumped at the chance to work for Aunt Jane in October. I didn't know much about typesetting, but I was a quick learner—and I knew for sure that it beat dragging that surveyor's chain around, hour after hour, day after day. I hadn't intended to make a career of the newspaper business. But before I knew it, I was shop foreman. When Aunt Jane went back east, I filled in as editor. When she decided not to return, I bought the paper and took over as publisher as well—for the next thirty years."

"Tell me a bit about Mrs. Swisshelm, if you would," Holmes suggested.

"Well, before she came to Minnesota, she was already one of the most famous women in America," Mitchell recalled. "She gained national prominence when she became the first female reporter to sit in the press gallery of the United States Senate. But she really made a name for herself during a ten-year stint as editor of the Pittsburgh Saturday Visiter, where she became a leading spokesperson for the abolishment of slavery.

"When her marriage began to fall apart, she left her husband and came to Minnesota, to be near her sister, Elizabeth—my mother. That, I believe, was in June of 1857.

"At the time," our host continued, "the village of St. Cloud actually consisted of three distinct settlements. Middle Town, where the bulk of the merchants are now, was settled first, mostly by German immigrants. Upper Town, also known as Acadia, became a home-away-from-home for Southern slaveholders, led by the transplanted Tennessean, Sylvanus P. Lowry. Lower Town, where we are now, was occupied by immigrants from northern Europe. Its proprietor was a New Englander named George Brott.

"Brott wanted to build his power base in Lower Town. The best way to do it, he figured, was to get more people to move there. This was before the granite quarries helped put St. Cloud on the map, so it wasn't an easy task. He decided to start a newspaper designed to lure more immigrants to the area. In Aunt Jane, he saw the big name he needed to attract attention.

He didn't give her much of a budget to work with, so she finally got me to help with the typesetting, and a neighbor boy, Wesley Miller, to work the press."

"But you weren't the first apprentices she hired, is that correct?" Holmes asked.

"No, she had a couple of young fellows before us," Mitchell said. "One of the Doherty boys, who lived next door to the news office, and a big Swede, named Mattson."

"I see," Holmes said, putting the tips of his fingers together in front of his chest. "Exactly when and where was this?"

"Less than a mile south of here, right across the river from the steamboat landing," Mitchell recalled. "There was a small wooden building, in the shape of a T, with the office sticking out in front, and a two-story dwelling attached to the back. Aunt Jane moved into the house and began editing the newspaper in January of 1858, I'm certain."

"The two boys you mentioned," Holmes asked, "they both worked for her from January until October of that year, when you returned from Breckenridge?"

"That's right," Mitchell confirmed.

"Do you know why she let them go?"

"As far as I know," Mitchell said, "it was a financial decision. As I said, Brott hadn't given her much of a budget. She got me to work for next to nothing, because I was family. And Wes, he came cheap because his pa shared Aunt Jane's political convictions. Wes was killed at Gettysburg, but his father, Stephen, went on to become governor of Minnesota, you know!"

"No, I didn't," Holmes said, as if not interested. "Getting back to the first two boys, Doherty and Mattson: How did they get along with each other?"

"Oh, they were thick as thieves, for years," Mitchell said. Then, as an afterthought, he added, "Until Zoe came between them."

"Zoe?" said Holmes, his interest picking up. "Who, or what, is Zoe?"

"Zoey was our nickname for my cousin, Mary Henrietta," Mitchell explained. "She's Aunt Jane's daughter."

"What can you tell me about her?" Holmes asked, a sense of urgency in his voice.

"Well, Zoe was only about six or seven when she moved here with her mother," Mitchell recalled. "That made her about half as old as I was. But at the time, there weren't any other girls her age around here, so she used to follow me everywhere. When I fished for catfish in the river, she'd wet a line, too—though she refused to use any bait. When I hiked up the ravine, she tagged along to pick wildflowers. I pretended not to like her, but over the years, we became quite good friends."

"Did she look like her mother?" Holmes asked pointedly.

"The spitting image," Mitchell replied.

"You say this girl was six or seven years old when she came here," Holmes pondered, "and as I understand it, your aunt moved back east the year after the Sioux Uprising. That would have made your cousin, what, eleven or twelve years old when she and her mother left?"

"Oh, no," Mitchell said. "Zoe didn't go back east right away. Her mother got involved as a nurse in the War Between the States, and then was bed-ridden with an illness for a couple of years after that. Zoe lived with my parents until she was almost eighteen."

"And when did your cousin, as you say, come between the two boys, Doherty and Mattson?"

"That would have been right before she moved back east to live with her father and grandmother," Mitchell said, sounding hesitant for the first time.

"Do you know the details?" Holmes asked.

"Not well enough to feel comfortable discussing them," Mitchell replied.

"It could be very important, to our mutual friend, Brower," Holmes urged.

"Then I suggest you talk with my mother," Mitchell said. "She lives right across the street. I'll walk you over there on my way back to work."

CHAPTER 19

DAYTON'S BLUFF

I did not accompany Holmes to the home of Henry and Elizabeth Mitchell. Instead, I went to visit Becky and her mother, as previously planned.

When I rejoined Holmes late that afternoon, aboard a train heading back to St. Paul, I naturally pumped him for information on what young Zoe Swisshelm might have done to cause the rift between our victim, Padraig Doherty, and the man who looked more and more to be the killer, Stig Mattson. Holmes quickly changed the subject.

"So tell me, Peter," he said, "all these church steeples we see on the horizon. Is one of them above the church where you'll be married?"

"Oh, no," I replied. "We're getting married at St. Peter's Catholic Church, in Browerville."

"Why there, if I may ask?"

"It's a long story," I said.

"We have more than an hour," Holmes said. He no longer wanted to talk about the case we were working, that was obvious. So I told him the whole story about the church.

Becky's mother was Roman Catholic. It was her dying wish that Becky be raised in the Catholic faith as well. The Browers honored that wish, even though they were Episcopalian. When it came time to plan our wedding, Becky wanted to be married in a Catholic church. The only problem was, I wasn't Catholic. As a result, the priest said he would be happy to perform the ceremony in a private home (as then-Father John Ireland had been so eager to do nearly thirty years earlier, for the young Mary Mehegan, a devout Roman Catholic, and the up-and-coming

James J. Hill, a now-and-then Methodist), but he could not marry us in a Catholic church. That's when Superintendent Brower stepped in.

The town of Browerville's first settlers were Poles, who established St. Joseph's Catholic Church in the early 1880s. The next wave of immigrants came from Germany. The German Catholics worshiped side-by-side with the Poles for a decade or so, before they decided they wanted their own church. By 1895, they'd established St. Peter's Catholic Church.

As it turns out, Browerville was not yet large enough to support two Catholic churches. Both were struggling financially. When Brower learned that one of the elders at St. Peter's was also a member of the local school board, he came up with a plan. In addition to agreeing to donate land for a new public school (which he'd planned to do anyway), Brower offered to make a significant contribution to the coffers of the struggling new church—as long as his daughter was allowed to hold her wedding there. It was an offer the good Father Stanislaus and his congregants could not afford to refuse.

Some would have called it blackmail. Archbishop John Ireland definitely would not have approved. But St. Peter's Catholic Church belonged to the Diocese of St. Cloud, which had recently had its differences with the Archdiocese of St. Paul. St. Cloud's beloved Bishop Marty had passed away in September. Though it had been three months now, Archbishop Ireland had not yet gotten around to naming a replacement. Across much of the diocese, impatience had fostered resentment, which eventually festered into defiance. So, a Catholic church wedding it would be (albeit one without a Mass).

As I'd anticipated, the story seemed to bore Holmes—who at last was ready to talk about our case. "Mrs. Mitchell's story contains circumstances that might lead a jury to sympathize with Stigvard Mattson," Holmes told me, without revealing any further details. "I believe if I can explain this to Mattson, I might be able to convince him to turn himself in to the authorities."

"So, you want one more shot at getting inside his head," I replied.

"Yes," Holmes said, "tonight, before O'Connor gets his mitts on the man."

"At Foley's?" I asked.

"No, the billiards league is off tonight," Holmes replied. "Foley is having a private holiday party for his employees and their families. It's closed to the public. I expect that, by the time we get to St. Paul, Mr. Mattson will be home for the night."

"Are you going to notify Chief O'Connor of your intentions?" I asked.

"Not yet," Holmes said. "The Bull seems to have a way of always putting things in the worst light. Based on what I've learned today, I'd like to give Mattson a chance to come in on his own terms. If he doesn't agree to surrender peaceably, then I'll have to take him by force."

"Are you sure that's wise?" I asked. "Remember, you once underestimated Peter Neunen. You could be doing the same with Mattson."

"That, my friend, was one of those instances where there were many things going on of which you were not aware," Holmes admonished me. "But you do have a point. I'll give you credit, Peter, your presence has come in handy more than once in the past. Since you do have some experience in such matters, you'll be happy to know that I have a backup plan that does involve you."

"Alright!" I said enthusiastically. "Let's hear it, then!"

Holmes said that the train would slow down considerably once we reached the St. Paul city limits. This would allow him to jump off near the Hamm's Brewery, and approach Mattson's shack from the north. I was to stay on the train until it passed Railroad Island, then disembark at East Seventh Street, to take up my post at the Improvement Arches. In effect, we would be sealing off Swede Hollow at both ends, trapping Mattson in the middle.

I did see one flaw. "There are two railroad tunnels through the bridge," I said. "How am I supposed to watch them both?"

"That's where Herr Mueller comes in," Holmes answered.

"Mueller?" I asked. "How will we get hold of him?"

"He's sitting two rows behind you," Holmes replied.

So, that was the plan. When we reached the Seventh Street Improvement Arches, I was to hide in the shadows at the north end of the west tunnel, while Mueller would position himself at the south end of the east tunnel. If Mattson, for any reason, were to run from Holmes, the man would likely try to escape to the south, forcing him to use one of the tunnels. If either Mueller or I spotted Mattson in our respective tunnel, we were to wait until he reached the midpoint. Then, we were to signal the other man to seal off the opposite end. Hopefully, we could keep the killer trapped until Holmes caught up with him again.

"Under no circumstances," Holmes warned, "must you try to tackle him alone. He's strong as an ox, after muscling beer kegs around all day. And remember, he's already killed one man."

Mueller seemed hurt by the suggestion that he might not be able to handle Mattson on his own. But he nodded in affirmation. I, for one, was glad to have him on our side!

Sure enough, things went just as Holmes predicted they would—up to a point.

Holmes jumped off the train as it passed the Hamm's Brewery. Mueller and I got off at East Seventh Street. From there, the German and I went our separate ways, he to the south side of the Improvement Arches, I to the north, where I chose my spot amid a brace of birch trees. I could see the entire mouth of the west tunnel, and much of the upper west side of the ravine. The trees that hid me from sight also blocked my view of the lower east side of the ravine, and the entrance to the east tunnel; but that's OK, they were Mueller's responsibility.

The night was dark and cold. Two nights before Christmas, and it was just like the story said: not a creature was stirring, not even a mouse. The stillness was eerie. Finally, after what seemed like two hours, I heard someone coming. The man was on a dead run. It had to be Mattson. I slid further into the shadows, and held my breath.

"Peter, are you there?" the man whispered. It was Holmes.

"Yes, I'm here," I said, emerging from the shadows.

"Mattson, did you see him?" he asked.

"No, not a sign of him," I said. "What happened?"

"He confessed to everything," Holmes said. "He said he'd come with me peaceably, even offered to retrieve the murder weapon for me. When I least expected it, he locked me in his shack and took off. I had little trouble getting out, but he was gone."

"Well, he didn't enter my tunnel," I said confidently.

Just then, we heard Mueller yell, from the far end of the second tunnel.

We raced through the east railroad tunnel to the south side of the Improvement Arches. When we emerged, we could see Mueller scrambling up the western foothill, twenty or more yards behind Mattson. At the top of the hill, Mattson jumped on a cable car that had just left Payne Avenue. Mueller reached the tracks and raced after the trolley, barely managing to climb aboard the electric car it was towing up the hill. Before it could make it all the way across the Arches, the electric car ground to a halt. Mattson had uncoupled it from the cable car!

Holmes and I worked our way across the bridge to Mueller's position in the trolley. The last we saw of Mattson, he was scuffling with the ticket-taker, as their cable car proceeded up Dayton's Bluff.

CHAPTER 20

THE CAVES

"I'm sorry," Mueller said, when Holmes and I reached him. "He snuck up on me while I was having a smoke. He must have recognized me from Foley's, and bushwhacked me."

"Don't worry, we'll get him," Holmes said. I wasn't so sure. As Holmes himself had pointed out, now that Mattson had been spooked, there was nothing to keep the man from leaving St. Paul, or all of Minnesota, for that matter.

Nevertheless, the three of us hoofed it up to the top of the hill, where the cable car had stopped. There, we spoke to the conductor, who'd also been roughed up by Mattson. "He headed that way," the man said, pointing down Maria Avenue.

"To the brewery," Holmes predicted, and we were off.

Sure enough, when we reached Jacob Schmidt's North Star Brewery, we found a spot out back where someone had slid down the hill in the snow.

"He's going to the caves," Holmes said. And so were we.

At the bottom of the steep hill, it didn't take us long to find the entrance to a cave, right beneath the brewery. The cave's mouth was about five feet tall, and twenty-five to thirty feet wide. Once inside, out of the moonlight, we were in pitch dark.

Mueller, the smoker, lit a match. Rats scurried everywhere. There were old, wooden beer kegs scattered all around the cavern. Holmes picked one up and, in the dark, smashed it against the rocks. When Mueller lit another match, Holmes picked up three broken staves, handing one to each of us. "Here," he said, "use these as torches."

Unfortunately, the barrel staves were damp. We couldn't get them lit.

"Douse the ends with this," Holmes said, pulling a bottle from his pocket.

"What is it?" I asked.

"Fuel from Mattson's shanty," Holmes explained. "I took it to use as evidence."

"Won't you need it in court?" Mueller asked

"There's plenty more where this came from," Holmes replied. "Mattson must have stocked up extra, to help him make it through the long holiday weekend. Besides, if we don't catch him, any evidence will be irrelevant."

Once we had three torches lit, we got a better look at the cave. At the back of the main cavern, opposite the entrance, there were openings to three more chambers. We decided to split up, each of us taking a different route: Holmes in the middle, me to the left, Mueller to the right. Again, Holmes cautioned the two of us to be careful, and to signal the others at the first sign of trouble. "Don't try to be a hero," he warned.

He didn't need to worry about me! I'm not afraid to admit it: I was scared. I wasn't crazy about being underground in the first place. I was already tired of the dampness, and I didn't like the rats, or bats. I'd also heard tales about the caves being haunted by ghosts of Indians who'd been buried nearby. To calm myself, I began to whistle. Who cares if the murderer heard me? If anything, I hoped my whistling would chase Mattson into the arms of Holmes.

I'd inched my way into my cave maybe thirty yards, when my whistling began to echo. Soon, the echoes had echoes! It was obvious that I was entering a much larger cavern, with many nooks and crannies. Thank goodness my torch was still going strong!

As I emerged from a small passageway into a much larger one, the ground suddenly went out from under me. I fell to a ledge about ten feet below. I had dropped my torch, which kept falling, for what seemed like several seconds, before I heard a splash. Then it went out. I was in total darkness.

I felt above me with my hands, to see if there was any way I could climb out. There was not. Slowly, I began to shuffle my feet around, to see if I could move left or right. I could not. I was trapped, who knows how many feet above an ice-cold underground spring. Finally, I began to yell for help. I got no answer.

After what seemed like an eternity, I thought I saw a glimmer of light above me. I began yelling again. The light got brighter. "Holmes, is that you?" I asked hopefully.

"No such luck, kid," I heard a voice say. A torch-lit face peered over the ledge above me. It was Mattson. "Can you swim?" he asked.

"Yes," I replied, which apparently was a mistake.

"Then you're on your own," he said. And he was gone.

Again, I started yelling for help. Sooner than I expected, I saw another glimmer of light. Had Mattson's conscience gotten the better of him, bringing him back to save me?

"Peter, is that you? Are you alright?" Better yet, it was Holmes!

"I'm alive," I said. "But I really wanna get out of here!"

He came to the edge of the ledge and reached down toward me. I stretched up as high as I could. We were barely able to clasp hands. "I can't get enough leverage to pull you up," he said, after several minutes of trying. "We'll have to use my coat as a rope."

"Hurry," I said. "Mattson was here, just moments ago. You don't want to lose him again."

"I'd rather lose him for the time being than lose you forever," Holmes said. He tied a knot in one sleeve of his old box coat and lowered it down to me. As he tugged on the other sleeve, I was able to pull myself up to safety.

"Let's get out of this hellhole," I said, as soon as I had my feet back on solid ground. When we finally exited the cave, I reveled in the fresh, open air. "I've never been so glad to see the moon and the stars!"

Suddenly, we heard yelling above us. It sounded like Mueller the Mauler. As Holmes and I moved out onto the river flat, away from the mouth of the cave, we could see two silhouettes on the bluffs above. In the moonlight, we could tell it was Mueller, chasing Mattson toward the old Indian burial grounds just south of the brewery.

As Mattson scurried toward the top of one of the mounds, Mueller did just what he'd been told not to do. He tackled the man on his own. As they both rose to their feet, the big Swede delivered a powerful left hook that sent the German tumbling off the mound.

"Let's go!" Holmes said, reaching from tree branch to tree branch to pull himself up the steep cliff. "If we're lucky, Mueller can stall him until we get there to help."

Sure enough, when we had finally struggled our way to the top of the bluff, we could see the two men still duking it out atop yet another Indian mound. By now, Mueller was successfully dancing circles around his opponent, jabbing him with punch after punch, while managing to avoid any blows similar to the one that had sent him sprawling earlier. Mattson was unable to hurt the man, yet unable to escape. Once he saw he'd been surrounded, the Swede threw up his arms in defeat, and Holmes put the cuffs on him.

"Nice comeback," Holmes said to Mueller. "What happened with that first punch?"

"I forgot for a moment that he was left-handed," Mueller said, rubbing his jaw.

"I was afraid that was the end of it, right there," I said, about Mattson's opening blow.

"One thing about Mueller the Mauler: I can take a punch," the German said, with pride. "Forty bouts without a knockout."

"Make that forty-one," Holmes said, raising Mueller's right arm to signal a winner.

The old pugilist grinned, his chipped front teeth glistening in the moonlight.

CHAPTER 21

A CONFESSION

Early Thursday morning, we met with Chief O'Connor to hear Mattson's confession. Brower was invited, because it was his skin that had been on the line. Holmes had also arranged for me to attend, in the official capacity as a new cub reporter for the St. Paul Dispatch. It was to be my first scoop!

As the chief of detectives had already told us, Padraig Doherty and Stigvard Mattson had been neighbors, growing up together near the river in St. Cloud. The little Irishman was a couple of years older, but the young Swede was big for his age, so they became fast friends.

As we learned from William Mitchell, when Jane Grey Swisshelm took over the St. Cloud Visiter, the two neighbor boys both went to work for her in the newspaper office. Doherty was good with numbers and letters, and soon became the stick boy, helping to set type in the composite stick.

Mattson was never good at that kind of stuff, but he provided the muscle, loading, unloading and moving around the reams of paper, barrels of ink, heavy press plates, and so on. He even rolled the plates for the press. So they all became a team, the pioneering newspaper lady, and her two young apprentices.

Mattson picks up the story from there. "Mrs. Swisshelm and Sylvanus Lowry were at each other, right from the git-go," he recalled. "At first it was the slavery issue. Being from Tennessee, he was for it. She was dead set against it. Then it was politics. He supported Buchanan. She didn't. She also got into a name-calling match with the wife of his lawyer."

There were threats made against the newspaper, and against Mrs. Swisshelm herself.

"One night, in March or April of 1858," Mattson went on, "Lowry himself, his shyster lawyer, and one of the lawyer's shirttail relatives came to the office to destroy the press.

"Me and Paddy, probably ten and twelve at the time, were out back of the office having a chew. Paddy, he kind of shied away a bit, as usual. But me, I knew I was going to quit school as soon as I was of age. I also knew that General Lowry had connections. I figured that if I could impress Lowry, he'd give me a job—a real one.

"While Paddy cowered in the corner, I whaled into that press with a sledge hammer just like the rest of 'em. Then I loaded up a big box of type and threw it in the river. We all laughed, except Paddy, who was scared to death. Even though I was younger, I was still bigger, so I told him I'd whup him if he ever said a word to anybody. An' he kept his mouth shut about it for years, outta fear, I suppose.

"Anyhow, we all moved on to other things and forgot about it, or so I thought. As the years went by, little Nettie, Mrs. Swisshelm's daughter, started to grow into a young woman, and a right purty one at that. I'd always been kinda sweet on her, but I never did nothing about it, outta respect, or maybe it was fear, too, of Lady Jane.

"But after the Sioux Uprising was put down, in 1863, Mrs. S headed east, to campaign for severe punishment against the Indians, leaving Nettie behind with an aunt and uncle. And that's when I saw my chance to tell her how I felt. Lady Jane got involved in nursing and decided to stay out east until the War was over, so during the next couple years, Nettie and me fell in love and started talking about marriage, even though she was barely in her teens.

"But Paddy, he musta been kinda sweet on Nettie, too, cuz he got real upset when I told him about it. At first, he just laughed and ridiculed me. When he saw that Nettie was just as serious about me, he threatened to tell everyone about my role in trashin' the Visiter. I didn't think he'd really do it, and even if he did, I didn't think it would make no difference after that many years. But next thing I knew, Nettie refused to see me, and within a few days she had packed up and moved east to join her Pa, without so much as a word of goodbye."

Mattson paused for a moment, then continued. "Paddy claimed he'd had his way with her before she left. I didn't believe that either, not after she'd denied me intimacy many times, saying she'd been brought up to save that sort of thing for marriage. I wrote letters to her for months, but never got a reply. Paddy left town about the same time, but he'd gone in the other direction, to Fargo, I heard. Never saw or heard from either one of them for years.

"Then, about ten years ago, Lady Jane died, and of course her obit was in all the papers. Mary Henrietta was listed as a survivor, so I sent her a sympathy card. To my surprise, she replied with a nice thank-you note. After a few months of correspondence, she finally told me why she'd left. Never mentioned a word about what happened at the Visiter. Said that Paddy had, indeed, forced himself upon her, and afterward she felt so dirty and ashamed that she couldn't face me, and after she moved off, she didn't know how to tell me, so she never answered any of my letters.

"After a while, I had quit writing, and she had eventually married someone else. I never did, though. She was the love of my life, and I never got over her. But I grew to hate my old friend, Paddy, and to blame him for my lot in life.

"Then, a couple weeks ago, I heard he was back in town. I learned he'd lost a leg, and had turned to drink, so he wasn't too hard to find. I thought I spotted him one night down by the levee, but I was with pals, so I didn't approach him. The next night I went back alone, but he wasn't there. It was the start of that cold snap, and I figured he musta found a warm place to stay. A couple nights later, I spotted him again, and followed him to the Ryan's courtyard, where he slipped in through a basement window. I could see I was too big to go in that way, so I counted windows to figure out which part of the building he was in, then went around and snuck in the other side. The night watchman was asleep, so that part was easy.

"I went into the basement, found the room I figured he was in, and broke in the door. Sure enough, there he was, trying to get out of the cold. He was liquored up, but he recognized me right away. I asked him about Nettie, and he cackled; said, sure, he'd had his way with her, then started to tell me all about it.

"I grabbed the nearest thing I could find off a shelf and clobbered him with it. I was so mad, I hit him so hard, I was sure he was dead. To cover my tracks, I dumped a bunch of papers in the middle of the floor, and set them afire, using a bottle of fuel I'd snuck out of the brewery to heat my shack."

"That, I'm afraid, was your undoing," Holmes had told him. "You stepped in the fuel and left two footprints at the scene. Analysis of the residue led us to the brewery, and eventually to you. The photo in your watch case helped us discover your link to the victim. It was fairly elementary, really—though a bit time-consuming to go through all the steps."

"I wondered how you found me so fast," Mattson said. "You know, I never meant to set the whole place on fire, just Paddy. From what I heard, the elevator shaft sucked the flames all the way up to the roof, and then the fire just burned its way back down. I'm real sorry about Mr. Brower's papers, and for all the trouble I caused everybody else. But Paddy, he got what he deserved."

"And you'll get what you deserve, which will be the rest of your life in prison," said Bull O'Connor. "But first, tell us what you did with the sword."

"Well, I took it from the scene with me, of course," Mattson said. "I ain't that dumb! I figured it might be worth something, especially with that ivory handle and all. But after I got it home in the candlelight, and seen Mr. Brower's name and initials all over it, I knew that plan wasn't gonna fly. So I got rid of it, someplace I figured nobody would ever look for it."

"And where might that be?" O'Connor asked.

"On the bank of Phalen Creek, right under the Oleson's privy," Mattson said. "What with all their kids, plus grandparents and aunts and uncles, there must be fifteen of 'em living in that shack. I figured by morning, the evidence would be covered in—"

"We get the picture," the lawman said, cutting him off. "I believe retrieving that particular item will be the perfect job for a certain young foot patrolman I know."

We all shared a snicker as we pictured young Daniel O'Harra searching for the murder weapon, by now waist deep in human excrement. O'Connor then told Brower that he could have his sword and scabbard back within a few days.

"Based on this confession," the Bull said, "I don't think we'll need to bring that evidence to trial. Superintendent Brower, you're free to enjoy the holiday and your daughter's wedding—thanks to Mr. Holmes, and young Peter here."

"Thanks to you, too, Chief," Holmes said. "I'm sorry you had to waste your valuable time on the likes of Johnny Tomasko."

"Oh, that wasn't a waste of time at all," O'Connor said with a grin. "When we brought Johnny's cronies in and accused them all of conspiracy in a murder case, they started to sing like canaries. It turns out that Tomasko was ringleader of the South Side Bucket Brigade."

"The Bucket Brigade, what's that?" Brower asked.

"A gang of thugs who hang out at the Bucket of Blood saloon," the Bull explained. "They tried to establish a protection racket in the Irvine Park neighborhood, offering to guard wealthy homeowners from vandalism, and promptly burglarizing the homes of anyone who refused to pay the price. The night Padraig Doherty was killed, Tomasko and his henchmen were busy robbing the Rudawski residence. Once we rounded them up, they all took turns ratting on each other, and they'll all do time. We've already recovered most of the stolen property to use as evidence. So don't feel sorry for me!

"Besides," the Bull added, "as I understand it, it was my man, Mueller, who was actually responsible for your fugitive's capture."

"Yes, I'm sure Peter's newspaper report will speak with great regard of Herr Mueller's role, as well as your wisdom in putting him on the case," Holmes said. And, of course, it did.

CHAPTER 22

WEDDING DAY

I barely had time to file my first report for the Dispatch, before I caught a train to Willmar to meet my family at Uncle Dan's for Christmas Eve. Superintendent Brower headed directly to his home in St. Cloud, where we all joined him on Christmas Day. All of us, that is, except for Holmes. That was another story.

Holmes had been invited, of course, to join my family for Christmas. He'd also been invited to accompany Brower back to St. Cloud. True to his nature, he declined both invitations.

"I think I'll stick around St. Paul another day or two," he explained. "I've heard so much about this man, Ireland, that I can't leave town without seeing him in person. Anyone who has obtained such a prominent position must be a powerfully persuasive speaker. I'd like to hear it for myself.

"Based on experience," Holmes added, "I expect the churches will be so crowded Christmas morning, it should provide a perfect opportunity for me to slip in and out unnoticed."

I did not see Holmes again until Saturday morning. I was in a dark little wikiup on Lake Charlotte, trying to harpoon a big northern pike with the new spear Uncle Dan had given me for Christmas, when Holmes peeled back the flap.

"They told me I'd find you here," he said.

"How was your Christmas?" I asked him. "Did you get to hear Archbishop Ireland?"

"Yes, I did, at the old cathedral on Sixth and St. Peter," Holmes said. "He drew quite a crowd, and was rather impressive, though a bit long-winded for my liking. By the way, you'll never guess who I ran into on my way out of church."

"Bull O'Connor?" I offered.

"A good guess," Holmes said, "but, no. It was James J. Hill, along with his wife, most of his children, and even a grandchild or two. While his family socialized with other congregants, Hill pulled me aside for a private chat—the gist of which I'll have to share with Superintendent Brower, if I get the chance. If not, I hope you'll pass the message on to him someday?"

"Sure," I said. "What's the message?"

"Hill confessed that, as much as he likes to rankle Brower about his passion for rivers, truth be told, Hill's own greatest accomplishment would not have come about had it not been for another search for the source of a river, by a young man with the same passion as Brower."

"How's that?" I asked.

"He was referring to his quest to turn the Great Northern into a transcontinental railroad, to compete with the Northern Pacific. He knew that whichever railroad reached the Northwest with the straightest track, over the lowest grade, would be the one that ended up with the fewest empty boxcars. So it was imperative for him to find a pass through the Rocky Mountains.

"As it turned out, a young engineer named John Stevens saved Hill's railroad line nearly twenty-two hundred feet in elevation, and hundreds of thousands of dollars, by tracing the Marias River to its source on the continental divide. Ironic, isn't it?" Holmes asked.

"Indeed," I replied. "I've never heard that story before. I'm sure the Superintendent hasn't either, or he certainly would have shared it with me. I look forward to telling it to him."

"Great," Holmes said. "Now, Peter, tell me a bit about your in-laws, whom I've only just met. Have your folks met them before?"

"Oh, yes," I said. "Both families got together for a picnic in July, when the Browns Valley Brass Band played at a Minneapolis Millers game at their new ballpark on Nicollet Avenue. And over Thanksgiving, Ripley went out to Browns Valley with me to do some hunting."

"He's a sportsman, then?" Holmes asked.

"Yeah, he played football and baseball in college," I replied. "He still plays a little baseball, but he's really big into fishing and hunting. They say he's destined for a future in politics, but

I can't imagine him leaving his law practice in St. Cloud to head down to the big capital city. He likes the rural life too much, I think."

"What about your sister-in-law, Josephine?"

"Josie's a school teacher—one of the best around, from what I hear—and real smart. She graduated from St. Cloud Normal at the age of sixteen, their youngest graduate ever! She found a job teaching in Willmar right away, then moved to Duluth, and is now in the Twin Cities. She's very creative, gifted in art, music, poetry, dance, you name it."

"Are either of them married?" Holmes asked.

"Not yet," I replied. "I'm sure Rip has had plenty of chances. He has a lot of lady friends, he just hasn't found the right one yet. Josie is so busy, I don't think she has much time for men."

"Too bad," Holmes said. "She's quite attractive."

"Yeah, Josie gets those dark eyes and high cheekbones from her mother," I said. "Russian, you know."

"Mrs. Brower seems like a lovely lady," Holmes replied. "But your fiancée reminds me more of your own mother."

"Thanks—I think," I said.

"Yes, it was intended as a compliment, very much so," Holmes confirmed.

"What about you?" I asked. "Are there any important women in your life—other than Swedish language tutors?"

"No," Holmes said, with a chuckle. "Most of the women I run across are not the type you want to take home to Mother. It's a hazard of the profession, I guess."

"Too bad," I said. We sat quietly for several minutes, watching for fish through the hole in the ice. It was approaching time for me to get ready for the wedding. We'd rented the banquet hall at the Reichert Hotel in Long Prairie for our reception that night, and had a couple of rooms there as well. That's where the bridal party was assembling.

"Well, I'd better head back to the group," I said. "Before we go, I have a gift for you."

I dug into my box of tackle and pulled out a wooden fish decoy. "Red Thunder carved it for me. I thought you might like to have it, as a souvenir of your trip to Browns Valley. I wanted to give it to you ten years ago, but you left town without saying goodbye."

"I apologize for that, Peter," he said. "Again, it was one of those instances in which there were circumstances of which you were not aware. But I thank you for the gift. I have one for you as well, but you'll have to wait until this afternoon to see what it is."

"Can you give me a hint?" I asked.

"Sorry," he said. "It's a surprise."

"That's not fair!" I protested.

"I promised your fiancée that I'd keep it a secret, the night we dined at the White House, remember?" he asked. "Besides, I suspect that you've been keeping a secret from me too!"

With that, he left the wikiup, closing the flap behind him.

I was not sure if I would ever see him again. He wasn't a great one for goodbyes. I did not see him when I returned to the Reichert to get dressed up, nor did I see him when I arrived at the church. By that time, I had more important things to worry about.

Before I knew it, the boys from the brass band were playing the Trumpet Voluntary up in the choir loft. Ripley and Josie escorted their mother to her front-row seat, then took their places at the altar. Then it was my turn. I walked arm-in-arm with Ma and Pa to their seats, then took my place at the altar.

As Father Stanislaus and the altar boy followed next, I stood and listened to the music. Remembering that the brass band would play the Prince of Denmark's March on the way out, the thought came to me that Holmes would get a kick out of that. Then it occurred to me that I had not seen him since early that morning. Where the devil was Holmes? Had he skipped out again without saying goodbye?

It was now time for Jacob Brower to escort his daughter down the aisle. On the organist's cue, we all turned to face the back of the church. Afraid I might tear up with joy, I glanced up at the choir loft. As Sister Armella began to play the opening strains of Pachelbel's Canon, Holmes emerged from the shadows to join her on the violin.

"What a perfect gift!" I thought to myself. "He knows how much Becky and I love music. So this was his big surprise!"

Then I had to remind myself of his parting words that morning. There was an even bigger surprise yet to come, one that very few of us knew about—though Holmes, apparently, had figured it out: As my darling Becky marched proudly down the aisle to become my bride, she was already eight weeks pregnant with our first child.

THE END

This book is a work of historical fiction. Many of the people, places and events in the story are factual. Others are not. Following is a brief summary.

Sherlock Holmes is a fictional character created by Sir Arthur Conan Doyle. Fictional characters invented by the author of this book include: Peter Smith, Rebecca Louise Brower, Daniel O'Harra, Padraig Doherty, Stigvard Mattson, Hermann Oberhauf, Klaus Mueller, Johnny Tomasko and Otto the bartender.

The following are real people, though their participation in this story is entirely fictional: Jacob V. Brower, Armina (Shava) Brower, Ripley and Josephine Brower, James J. Hill and his family, Archbishop John Ireland, John "Bull" O'Connor, Josiah Chaney, Nels Sandberg, Theodore and William Hamm, Jacob Schmidt, Adolph Bremer, Jane Grey Swisshelm, Mary Henrietta Swisshelm, Thomas Lowry, Alfred Hill, Sylvanus Lowry, "Nina Clifford" (not her real name) and William B. Mitchell (not the same William Mitchell for whom the College of Law in St. Paul is named).

The December 1896 fire that struck lowertown St. Paul's Schutte Building and the Ryan Hotel Annex, and destroyed much of Jacob Brower's life work, was real. The "discovery" of a dead body in the ashes (along with everything that springs from it) is fictional. The stories about Jane Grey Swisshelm are true, with the exception of her (and her daughter's) involvement with the fictional characters Doherty and Mattson.

Most of the places in the book are real. Many of them still exist, and can be toured by the public. The August Schell Brewery in New Ulm and the James J. Hill Mansion, Indian Mounds Park, the Seventh Street Improvement Arches and nearby Swede Hollow in St. Paul, are just a few examples. If interested, you are encouraged to contact your state or county historical society for more information. The Minnesota Historical Society's website at www.mnhs.org is a great place to start.

ABOUT THE AUTHOR

Jeff Falkingham is a mystery lover and history buff who writes for readers of all ages who share those passions. His hometown of Browns Valley, Minnesota, was the setting for his first work of historical fiction, *Sherlock Holmes and the County Courthouse Caper*. This second book, *Sherlock Holmes: In Search of the Source*, is a sequel, set ten years after the original.

Jeff's first-grade teacher, Lillian Korsbrek, told him tales about her great-grandfather, the famous Minnesota pioneer Joseph Renshaw Brown. His second-grade teacher, Nita Duffield, inspired him to be a writer. His third-grade teacher, Ann Swanke, furthered his interest in Minnesota history, and instilled in him the discipline he needed to succeed in life.

Jeff has a B.A. in mass communications from St. Cloud State University and an M.A. in community and organizational leadership from Augsburg College. He began his career as a sportswriter. For the past twenty-five years, he has worked in corporate communications, marketing and advertising, most recently with Northern Tool + Equipment in Burnsville, Minnesota. He and his wife Bonita reside in Eden Prairie, Minnesota, where they raised two children, Erik and Amy, both currently in college.

Author Jeff Falkingham stands in front of the Seventh Street Improvement Arches that link lowertown St. Paul with Dayton's Bluff. Beyond the railroad tunnels lies the Swede Hollow ravine, former site of a shantytown that was home to thousands of immigrants. (Photo by Erik Falkingham)

ACKNOWLEDGMENTS

Thanks to the knowledgeable and courteous staff at the Minnesota History Center in St. Paul for all their help. Ditto to the helpful members of historical societies in Ramsey, Stearns and Todd Counties, as well as my friends and supporters back in Browns Valley.

Thanks to my wife, Bonita, and my children, Erik and Amy, for their patience, understanding and advice. Thanks to my colleagues Randy Meyers for his work on the cover and interior design of this book, Stacey Osten for constructing my website (www.cccaper.com), and Rainer Schulz, not only for proofreading my manuscript, but also for his constant encouragement and support.

Thanks to the Sherlockians around the world who challenged and encouraged me to write this second book. Thanks to my mentor, Milt Adams of Beaver's Pond Press, who helped me get my start in this business.

Finally, thanks to the following writers, and the librarians who helped me find their books or articles:

Anderson, Philip J. & Dag Blanck. *Swedes in the Twin Cities*

Atkins, Annette. *Creating Minnesota: A History from the Inside Out*

Brower, Jacob V. *The Mississippi River and its Source: A Narrative and Critical History of the Discovery of the River and its Headwaters, Accompanied by the Results of Detailed Hydrographic and Topographical Survey*

"Browerville" @ *www.browerville.govoffice.com*

Brueggeman, Gary J. "Beer Capital of the State: St. Paul's Historic Family Breweries" @ *www.mbaa.com*

Chaney, Josiah B. "Sketch of J.V. Brower for North Dakota Historical Society"

Conzen, Kathleen Neils. *Germans in Minnesota*

129

"De La Vergne: Pioneers in the Refrigeration and Oil Engine Industry" @ baldwindiesels.railfan.net

Delta Kappa Gamma Society of St. Cloud State University. "Biographical Sketches of Minnesota Pioneer Teachers"

Diers, John W. "The Force That Shaped Neighborhoods 1890-1953: Sixty-Three Years of Streetcars in St. Paul" in *Ramsey County History*

Dobbs, Clark A. "A Brief History of Archaeology in Minnesota" @ *www.fromsitetostory.org*

Doyle, Sir Arthur Conan. *Scandal in Bohemia, Sign of the Four, Study in Scarlet*

"Early History of St. Paul," *St. Paul Dispatch*, December 19, 1896

Endres, Kathleen. "Jane Grey Swisshelm: 19th Century Journalist and Feminist" in *Journalism History*

Flanagan, John T. *Theodore Hamm in Minnesota: His Family and Brewery*

Folwell, William Watts. *A History of Minnesota, Vol. 2*

Junior Pioneer Association. "Tough Times: The Sometimes Fortunes of Boxing in Early Minnesota," in *Ramsey County History*

Keillor, Steven J. *Shaping Minnesota's Identity: 150 Years of State History*

Klinger, Leslie S. *Life and Times of Mr. Sherlock Holmes, John H. Watson, M.D., Sir Arthur Conan Doyle, and Other Notable Personages*

Lewis, Anne Gillespie. *Swedes in Minnesota*

Lewis, Theodore Hayes. *Northwestern Archaeological Survey, 1898*

Lindley, John M. *Celebrate Saint Paul: 150 Years of History*

Lowry, Goodrich. *Streetcar Man: Tom Lowry and the Twin City Rapid Transit Company*

Martin, Albro. *James J. Hill and the Opening of the Northwest*

McCarthy, Abigail. "Jane Grey Swisshelm: Marriage & Slavery" in *Women of Minnesota: Selected Biographical Essays*

"Minnesota" @ *www.history.com/encyclopedia*

Mitchell, William B. *History of Stearns County*

Neil, Donald F. & Anthony Demetriades. "The True Utmost Reaches of the Missouri: Were Lewis and Clark Wrong?" @ fwp.mt.gov/mtoutdoors

Nelson, Charles B. *The First 125 Years: A Historical Sketch of the Grand Commandery of Knights Templar of Minnesota*

Pierson, Michael D. "Between Antislavery and Abolition: the Politics and Rhetoric of Jane Grey Swisshelm" in *Pennsylvania History Quarterly*

Regan, Ann. *Irish in Minnesota*

Swisshelm, Jane Grey. *Half a Century*

Warner, Mary. "Who Gets Credit? Naming the Source of the Mississippi River" @ *www.morrisoncountyhistory.org*

Wills, Jocelyn. *Boosters, Hustlers & Speculators: Entrepreneurial Culture and the Rise of Minneapolis & St. Paul, 1849-1883*

Wingerd, Mary Lethert. *Claiming the City: Politics, Faith, and the Power of Place in St. Paul*

Printed in the United States
138762LV00002B/133/P